F
WIL

Williams, Carol
   Lynch.

The true colors of
   Caitlynne Jackson.

36535

$14.95

DATE			

The True Colors of

CAITLYNNE

JACKSON

The True Colors of CAITLYNNE JACKSON

Carol Lynch Williams

Delacorte Press

Published by
Delacorte Press
Bantam Doubleday Dell Publishing Group, Inc.
1540 Broadway
New York, New York 10036

Library of Congress Cataloging-in-Publication Data
Williams, Carol Lynch.
    The true colors of Caitlynne Jackson / Carol Lynch Williams.
        p.   cm.
    Summary: Twelve-year-old Caity and her younger sister, Cara,
must fend for themselves when their abusive mother storms out of
the house with a suitcase and doesn't come back.
    ISBN 0-385-32249-6
    [1. Child abuse—Fiction.   2. Abandoned children—Fiction.
3. Mothers and daughters—Fiction.   4. Sisters—Fiction.]
I. Title.
PZ7.W65588Tr   1997
[Fic]—dc20   96-24835
                                                                  CIP
                                                                   AC

The text of this book is set in 13-point Granjon.
Manufactured in the United States of America
February 1997
BVG   10   9   8   7   6   5   4   3   2   1

To my sweet girls:
Elise, Laura, Kyra
and Caitlynne

Special thanks to those who helped me win the battle: Mary Cash, Drew Williams, Samantha Lynch, Tom Wallace, Bruce Aufhammer, Louise Plummer, Alane Ferguson, Bob Stein, Scott Welling, Rick Walton, Cheri Earl and Dave Cannon.

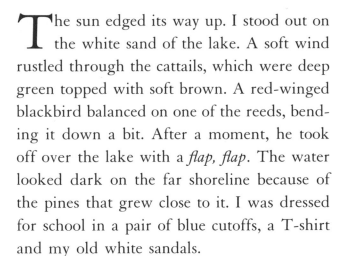

CHAPTER

ONE

The sun edged its way up. I stood out on the white sand of the lake. A soft wind rustled through the cattails, which were deep green topped with soft brown. A red-winged blackbird balanced on one of the reeds, bending it down a bit. After a moment, he took off over the lake with a *flap, flap*. The water looked dark on the far shoreline because of the pines that grew close to it. I was dressed for school in a pair of blue cutoffs, a T-shirt and my old white sandals.

I had tapped my sister awake, and she stood beside me in her to-the-knees nightgown. Cara's honey-blond hair hung tangled down her back; it was especially ratty in one spot, where her head had rested on the pillow.

"Now watch," I said.

Cara looked hard where I pointed, to where the sun rose. The sky seemed pure gold over the tops of the trees.

She squinted beside me, and I touched her real soft, so soft she might not have even noticed. It made my arm warm where our skin met. And then the sun came up. Bright, strong, pushing its fingers of light out to Cara and me. Now that we could see the sun, it kept moving as if a string pulled it across the sky, burning a path before and behind itself. As if it pointed to where it headed and, at the same time, showed where it had been.

"I wanna be able to draw that," I said. I gestured to the sunrise. Thin clouds changed from cotton white to pink, and back again to white.

Cara nodded. Then she squatted on the sand and started poking the ground with her finger. She bent over, her long hair covering her face. I knelt beside her. She looked at me. Her eyes were dark green.

"Last night I dreamed that Mom drowned." Cara glanced at me real quick and then back at the holes she had made.

"Oh," was all I could say.

"I was sitting on the slide, right by the top. The water was black. Mom kept going up and down in it. And then she went down for good."

I looked over to the slide, which stood in a place that should be shallow because of its nearness to the shore. We had it pointing to a hole where a spring bubbled. The water there was deep, so when we came off the slide we were in over our heads.

Cara leaned close to me. Her voice sounded soft. "Caity, I didn't even try to help her."

"Don't worry about it," I said, "because fat don't sink."

"She's got bones and guts in there," Cara said.

"Plenty of both," I said. "But mostly she's got fat. And anyway, I've never seen her do anything but float."

Mom's voice drifted down loud from our house, which was set up a ways from the lake on a small hill. "Miss that bus and it's a long walk, Cara. Tell your sister what I said."

Cara didn't. Instead she smiled at me. I couldn't remember why Mom wasn't talking to me this time. We turned and jogged home.

The sun wasn't quite as bright as it had been. It always happened that way. The sun seemed to take away a little of its brightness a bit after it peeked over the trees in the mornings. I wondered if it rose that same way all over Florida. All over the United States. All over the world.

We jumped over the low white block wall, built

years before to keep alligators from getting up to the house. Then we went quietly onto the front screened-in porch and into our living room.

"I'll make breakfast," I said. "You hurry and get dressed."

Cara moved to get past me, then stopped sudden-like. I turned. Mom stood waiting.

"Brush your hair, Cara," she said. "Or I'll cut it off."

Then, without a word to me, she left, going out through the kitchen. I heard the back door slam shut. A moment after came the sound of our old Ford Escort. It died once, then ground out a few noises before it started up good and strong. When we heard Mom drive off, both Cara and I began moving again. I realized I had been holding my breath. I took in a big gulp of air. Then I went into the kitchen.

The counters were piled high with dirty dishes. Pots and pans. Old food. Leftovers. Glasses. Everything fought for a place to rest and waited for me to take care of it. The trash from the garbage can spilled onto the sticky linoleum. The cabinets stood open. Most were empty because we had managed to use all the dishes this time. And because there wasn't much food.

I rummaged through the fridge to see if I could find something to eat. We had some milk left. Bread and oleo. Was there any peanut butter? No. Honey? Yes, a little.

I got out the electric sandwich maker that Nana, our grandmother, had given us the Christmas before last. It felt grimy from old grease. Cheese that had turned brittle stuck in some of the grooves. I wiped the grill part off with my hand, then plugged it in. I spread four pieces of bread with oleo after checking for mold. There was only a little on one corner of two slices. I pulled it off and threw the small forest of green and gray at the garbage can. I missed. Then I put the bread on the grill and poured honey all over the two bottom pieces. I topped the bread, then slapped the sandwich maker closed. We could drink the milk from the jug since there were no clean glasses.

Cara came hurrying into the kitchen.

"Mmm," she said. "Smells good."

"Clear the table," I said. I waited for the red light on the machine to flicker off. That meant the sandwiches were brown and heated through.

Cara pushed the papers and books and dishes with dried-out food to one side. She wore a pair of pants that bagged on her small body. Cara is slight, barely big enough to be in sixth grade. Her bones are tiny, her feet are tiny, even her face is small.

Me, on the other hand, I am big. My size helps with

sports, but it can be embarrassing, too. I feel too big to be in the seventh grade and only twelve and a half. I'm as tall as some of the boys, and even challenge one teacher, as far as height goes. My hands are big, my feet are big. And my nose. Gol, my nose looks like an Olympic ski jump. Luckily my hair hides my ears.

"Different fathers, different looks," Mom always says.

There are some things about Cara and me that are the same. Our hair color, for example. Dark blond, with lots of gold highlights. And green eyes. Brandon Hill, the boy next door, calls them cat eyes.

And the way we like to read, that's the same.

And being afraid.

Cara doesn't know her crying at night wakes me up. And there's not a lot I can do, 'cause I'm scared, too.

CHAPTER

TWO

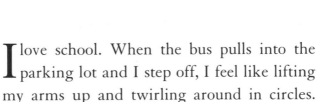

I love school. When the bus pulls into the parking lot and I step off, I feel like lifting my arms up and twirling around in circles. It's like I'm free or something. Of course I never do that. Twirl, I mean. But in my head that's what I'm doing.

Cara and I always go separate ways once we get to Oak Middle School. We don't have the same lunch or PE time, but I see her occasionally in the halls. We wave to each other but don't say much.

One of the things that I like about going to school is my two-hour art class. My other classes are good, too. I make Bs and Cs in all of them. But in art . . . there's just so much to do. So much color and paper and space to make things. If the bus arrives early, I go to the art room. Kathy Jordyn, my best friend, meets me there, and we talk and laugh until the bell rings.

As the bus bounced along toward school, I finished up my pre-algebra homework. Then I read some more of *Great Expectations*. It's an okay book. Not my favorite that we've read this year. I like the Newbery Award winners that Mr. Cannon let us choose ourselves. This Dickens guy is kind of long-winded.

We were pulling into the parking lot when three girls who live in my neighborhood walked back to where Cara and I sat together. It was Elaine Tuppers, Jennifer Franklin, and Mandy Wright. Their families have a lot of money. I'm not sure how it happened, but somehow our little log cabin got into the middle of a very rich neighborhood. I think our house was here first and everything else grew up around it. Anyway, Brandon Hill sat two seats up from us, and he turned and watched them.

"Look, Caity," said Jennifer. "If you'd wash your hair, you'd look a lot better." Jennifer is very pretty. There's no use wishing for anything she has. It's too expensive even to dream about.

"What?" I asked. I willed my face not to turn red. The bus bumped over a curb, and the three girls swayed with the movement. Now the kids in the seat near me were listening to Jennifer. Cara looked down at her feet and whistled a song with no real tune.

"I'm not trying to be mean," Jennifer said, and

Elaine and Mandy shook their heads to show that they weren't trying to be mean either. "But if you'd just try and keep clean, you'd look nicer. Maybe you'd have more friends."

"Oh." I wanted to say something else, but my mouth wouldn't work. I wanted to say, "I have plenty of friends." They're guy friends. I'm always out playing ball with the boys during lunch. And on Saturdays, too, on the one-acre lot that separates my house from Brandon's. I play second base and he pitches. Maybe having mostly guy friends doesn't matter in the seventh grade. If you're a girl, I mean.

Cara looked out the window then, and I glanced at my T-shirt. It was dirty.

Sometimes I am too tired, or, well, I just don't *want* to run my clothes through the washer and then hang them on the line. The bus stopped and the doors opened with a soft belch. Kids began to leave.

"Change your clothes every day and wash your hair twice a week," Jennifer said. I nodded and the girls turned to file away.

I could hardly move. Brandon still watched. Cara elbowed me in the ribs.

"Time to get off," she said.

My face felt all funny. Kind of how it might feel if I was frozen, I guess.

I scooted out and stood in the aisle.

As I walked past Brandon, he grabbed my wrist.

His hand was big and warm. I noticed his clothes were very clean looking.

"Caity," he said, "not everything's the same for everyone. You know what I mean?"

I didn't really, but I nodded anyway.

"See you in study hall," he said.

I moved away fast and walked to the large gray stucco building. I tried to blend in with the kids that were flowing from the parking lot into the school. Maybe then nobody would notice my shirt. Cara almost jogged, trying to keep up with me.

"You don't look that bad," she said. She touched me, briefly, on the arm.

"I just wish those girls could have told me at the end of school instead of at the beginning."

Cara nodded.

I ran ahead to art class.

CHAPTER
THREE

▼

Kathy was already in the art room. She wore a smock over her clothes and a pair of tight Levi's. She had braided her long black-brown hair. It fell over one shoulder. She leaned on the big table and colored in a pen-and-ink drawing she had done of an Arabian stallion. Kathy is good at drawing horses. She doesn't have one yet, because there's no room for them where she lives.

Kathy's nervous about visiting my place. She's never said she's afraid or anything, but lately she always has an excuse for not coming over. The acreage that goes with the house and lake isn't enough to make her want to spend the night, or even visit for an afternoon. I don't think my having a horse

11

would get her over more than the few times she has come.

She looked up from her artwork.

"Hey, Caity," she said. "What's the matter with you? You look like you're getting ready to bawl."

Kathy is from Atlanta, Georgia. Her father lives there now. She has a strong accent.

"Nothin'," I said, imitating her drawl. "Ah'm jus' fine." Somehow teasing my friend made me feel better. See, I thought, I do have friends.

"Are you coming over this summer?" I asked her. I got my painting from the cupboard, where I'd put it to rest after class the day before. It was a simple watercolor showing my lake at sunrise. I wanted to add the sun and maybe Cara and me on the white sand. There wouldn't be time to do any painting now. I'd have to wait for class. But I could sketch my sister and me in.

Kathy hesitated with her color work, then, flipping her braid back, said, "A week of school left and you're already lining up who's visiting."

"You know how quickly my guest list fills up." This was a joke. Except for Kathy and the ball playing, I'm not popular. I watched Kathy fidget and wondered if she'd come over.

"Well," she said at last. "I'll be going to Atlanta to stay with Jerry. Liza and he came to terms with that a night or two ago."

Liza and Jerry are Kathy's parents. They divorced two years ago.

"Well, when do you leave?"

"A week after school is out."

"Think you can come before you go?" I wasn't sure why I pushed her.

"I'll ask," she said after a pause. "But I think I'll have to be getting ready to leave. You know, packing and shopping. Stuff like that." She seemed relieved to have thought up an excuse.

"Be sure to call me when you get home," I said. "And write me the whole time you're gone."

"Of course," she said, and she smiled.

I smiled, too, then went to the large double sink at the back of the room and carefully washed my hands. They were a bit grubby. But not too bad, since I'd gone swimming the afternoon before. I pulled an apron over my head and tied it behind my back. With my shirt covered, I felt safer. Not so obvious.

I sat at the art table across from Kathy. We worked quietly, and I fell into my painting, becoming part of it. I lived the morning again through the picture, leaving out the messy kitchen and Cara's tangled hair. I left out the part of me wearing a dirty shirt, too.

At the sound of the morning bell, Kathy and I cleaned up our area. I tried to think of an excuse to wear my apron for the day, but one wouldn't come. After a few minutes of hemming and hawing, I hung the apron on a peg in the supply closet. Then we went to study hall together.

Far across the auditorium, I saw Brandon come in with his friends. He saw me and waved. Then he plopped into a chair. Devon Anderson shouted out, "Action Jackson," across the room at me. I wondered, from as far apart as we were, how dirty my shirt looked. Maybe I should have kept the apron on after all.

"He's cute, don't you think?" Kathy asked.

My face colored immediately. Had she seen me looking over at Brandon? *Did* I think he was cute? Enough girls at school did. In fact, right now, Jennifer was climbing over people's legs to get a seat near him.

I do like him, I realized. Could Kathy tell by looking at my face what my feelings were? I hoped she couldn't.

"Do I think who is cute?" I asked.

"Richard Bruce."

"You mean Richie Rich? Ah, he's okay. Not my type really."

"Muscles, money and good looks aren't your type? Come on, Caity." Kathy pushed at me.

"You've been reading too many of those teen magazines," I said. I sat in a chair and let my heavy books fall on my lap. Then I swung up the desktop so that it rested over me. "You sound like an ad for one of them."

Morning announcements crackled on over the intercom.

"And anyway," I said, lowering my voice, "Richie Rich doesn't have any muscles at all. He's just skin and bones. And nose."

Kathy laughed. "I like his nose. And he will have muscles. I can tell."

I do have to say this one thing about Kathy. She likes boys. I mean, really likes them, though no one would know it but her best friend. And she's real fickle. She says she gets that from her mom, which is why her parents divorced. Sometimes Kathy likes two or three different guys in one day. It makes me laugh.

I like guys okay. They're fun for baseball. And Brandon is cute. But right now I have too much on my mind to worry about boys.

"Let's work on French together," I said. "We've got that quiz today."

The room stayed quiet till after announcements; then a low hum filled the air. We can talk together if we're studying. Sometimes the noise gets out of hand, but I've gotten used to doing things with lots of yelling going on.

The day went as usual until computer class.

I had set myself down at my terminal when Brandon rushed in. His hair was wet from showering after gym. I touched my own dirty hair.

"Caity," he said. He slammed his books down near the terminal next to mine. He leaned in close to me. "I want to talk to you."

"Go ahead," I said, figuring he was planning to ask about starting a game for later, maybe after school.

"No, not here with everyone. Let's go out in the hall." Brandon glanced around, but nobody was looking our way. I looked around, too. What was he checking for?

"Oh, all right," I said. I hated to get up. I felt more visible, though most people just ignored me.

Brandon and I went out into the hall. Streams of kids ran this way and that. We moved up next to the wall, away from our classroom door.

"I was wondering," Brandon said. "If you'd like . . ." He paused.

"What?" I asked. "If I'd like what?"

He blushed.

What in the world could he be thinking? I wondered. I couldn't remember seeing him blush before. He was too, well, cocky for blushing.

"I heard what happened this morning. On the bus, I mean."

Now I turned red. "I'm trying not to think about it," I said. "Are we out here to make baseball arrangements or what?" I felt funny inside. Angry and embarrassed, both at the same time.

"Well, no, not exactly." Brandon shuffled his feet.

"Then we better get to class." Had I thought Brandon was cute only a few minutes before? I changed my mind right then and there.

"No, wait," Brandon said. He touched my arm real softlike. "I'm not trying to be mean. I only wanted you to know I never noticed any of the things Jennifer was saying."

I looked at him. Inside my heart was pounding hard. Don't cry, I thought. I willed the tears that were coming up fast to stay put. My eyes filled, but the tears never fell.

"What's the point, Hill?" When playing baseball, we always call each other by our last names. It made me feel tough and more in control.

He smiled a small smile. "Well, Jackson. I think you're all right."

"Thanks for the vote," I said. "Not that it matters any."

Mr. Bovie went into class, and I started after him. I needed to get away from Brandon, away from the whole school, but there wasn't anyplace to go, except my seat.

"Caity, wait." Brandon's voice was loud.

I turned back to him.

"Would you go to the dance with me?"

"What?" I asked, though I had heard him as plain as day. I stepped back to where he stood.

"This Friday night." He talked fast, running his words together. Was he always like this when he asked girls out? Or was it because it was me?

"Why? Do you feel sorry for me because of the bus thing this morning?" Now I was more angry than embarrassed, but I kept my voice low.

"No," Brandon said. "I wanted to do something with you. Something more than play ball. We always play ball. I thought we could do something different."

I stared hard at Brandon. Was he telling me the truth? My anger simmered down to nothing.

"You want to go to the end-of-the-school-year dance?" I asked. This was a very hard question to get out because my mouth was suddenly hanging open. And it was stupid. That's the only dance our school is having, what with there being so few days left in the year. My voice must have come out louder than I meant because two people walking close by heard and turned to look at Brandon and me.

"Yeah," Brandon said. And then he smiled. "If you want."

The hall sounds seemed to get even louder.

I felt embarrassed. I couldn't talk. Why did he ask me? Did he plan to make fun of me by telling all his friends? This wasn't Brandon at all, but my mind swirled with all the reasons he shouldn't be asking me to the dance. He usually does dance-type stuff with other girls. Girls like Jennifer.

"I, uh." I didn't have anything to wear. This was a dressy dance. And anyway, I am not a dancer. I mean, I have danced before, for my nana. Cara and I used to put plays on for her back when we visited. I danced then. I wondered if that would count.

My mind ran thick with reasons why going with him was not a normal thing. Brandon and I are just friends. Baseball-playing buddies. And then, Mom is always telling me what a big butt I have. Why would he want to go to the end-of-the-school-year dance with a big-butted, second-base-playing, dirty-haired, no-nice-dress, cannot-dance girl?

"Can you go? Do you think your mother would let you?" He leaned forward. I could smell some springy-type soap. It tickled my nose. I hoped I wouldn't sneeze.

The hall was clear now, except for the two of us. The bell rang. We moved toward the door.

"Why?" I whispered. "We don't do stuff like this."

"I'd like to go with you." He made it sound so simple.

My face burned now.

"Are you already going with somebody else?"

"Oh no," I said, embarrassed by that thought, too.

Mr. Bovie came to the door and leaned out to us. "You two think you'll be making it today?"

"Yes sir," I said, looking at the floor and hurrying to the room. Brandon and I bumped into each other as we tried to get to our seats. Everyone in class watched us. I hoped my ears wouldn't catch on fire; they felt that hot. I sat down. Brandon flopped into his own seat.

"What happened?" asked Marie Welch. She sits on the other side of me. We talk to each other a little, and work as lab partners sometimes, too.

"What happened when?" I asked.

"What did Brandon want?"

I looked over at Brandon. He looked at us both.

"Something private," I said.

Marie made her eyebrows jump up and down. "How private?"

Her face seemed to throb before my eyes. "So private it's none of your business," I said.

Marie's face got a squinchy look.

"Now that we have everyone here," Mr. Bovie said in a voice that seemed too loud, "let's get to work."

I felt like all eyes were on me. After a few moments I looked around. Only Brandon glanced at me.

Later at home, when I told Mom that Brandon Hill had asked me to the end-of-the-school-year dance, she looked at me openmouthed. Then she smiled.

"Well, isn't that real nice," she said, and it wasn't a question at all. "I wonder why?"

It felt like Mom had snapped my feelings with a rubber band, but I acted like it hadn't bothered me. "I wondered the same thing."

"Well, I know why," said Cara. "He likes you, Caity. You're tall and thin and pretty."

Mom snorted and laughed a little laugh. Then she said, "Well, I guess we'll have to go and get you a dress."

"What?" I asked. I couldn't believe it. My mouth hung open. "I didn't think we had the money."

"No, we don't," Mom said. "But I'll sacrifice something. I had planned to get Mother to make me a dress or two, but . . ." Mom waved her hand around in the air.

I looked at her billowy dress. Tiny yellow flowers ran a crazy pattern over the blue material. I suddenly felt sorry for Mom in her giant dress.

"I don't need anything," I said. "Maybe I can borrow from Kathy. She might have something I could wear."

Mom pulled at her tightly permed dark hair. "Maybe," she said.

"You're a lot taller than her, Caity," Cara said. "Whatever you got from her would be too short."

Mom heaved a sigh. She bit her bottom lip. "We'll

go to the Altamonte Mall tomorrow," she said. "Even though we can't afford it, we'll go to the mall."

That night I washed my waist-length hair in the kitchen sink with dish soap. I sat out in the evening and let the wind dry it.

"What beautiful tresses," Cara said, acting silly. She was on her way down to the lake. "O sweet maiden," she called, turning around and walking backward. "Wilt thou swim with thy dearest sister?"

"What are you reading in school?" I called back. "The Bible?"

"Come, maiden," Cara said, ignoring my question.

"It'll get my tresses wet," I said, but I ran down to the water, anyway, in my shorts and T-shirt. Cara and I played together till the sun sank and the night sky filled up with lightning bugs and the sound of crickets. Then we went to bed.

I put myself to sleep by dreaming of the dress I'd get the next day. It would be beautiful. It would minimize the size of my butt. It wouldn't be too big or too small. It would make me fit in at school with the girls, even if school was almost over. It was a nice dream.

On the bus the next morning Brandon motioned to me with his finger.

"Brandon wants you," Cara said. She leaned close. "Probably about that dance thing."

"Probably," I said. I was glad there were only a few people on the bus.

I went over to where he sat alone and sat behind him. He turned around, looking shyer than I could ever remember seeing him look.

"Well?" he asked. "Can you go?"

I nodded. "My mom said I could get a dress." My face was as red as a beet. "I'd like to go with you."

"That's cool," Brandon said. He breathed out a great big breath. Had he been worried I might say no? "It should be fun. I mean, I don't dance too good, but we'll do all right together, I bet." His face looked pink.

For some reason, seeing him embarrassed made me feel worse. I hate to see people struggling along, like when they have to give a book report or something. It's almost like doing it myself when I watch them.

I looked down at my hands, so good at drawing, terrific at catching a line drive, and didn't know quite what to do with them. Then I worried that my scalp was turning red, so I looked back up.

"The dance starts at eight, so I'll be over to pick you up a little before. My mom'll drive us." He looked out the window I sat next to when he talked.

"Okay," I said.

Then he smiled, the Brandon smile I knew from playing games, and stood up. "See ya in school."

I tried to smile back, but I think my lips quivered. Dates are definitely different than baseball.

He walked up to the middle of the bus.

After a moment, I went to sit back with Cara. She looked at me.

"Try not to act so nervous next time he talks to you."

"What makes you think I was nervous?"

"Your lips were shaking."

CHAPTER

FOUR

Mom was waiting for us at the bus stop when we got home from school.

"Get in. We're going to the mall," she called through the car window. The bus roared off with the smell of diesel and a twirling of sand and leaves.

Cara and I climbed into the Escort. My stomach did a flip-flop. This might be fun. I'd never shopped at the mall with my mother before.

"I thought we could make a day of it," Mom said, grinding the car into gear. "Shopping. Dinner. Maybe even a movie."

We shopped until I was tired, going from store to store. Every dress I liked, Mom hated and refused to buy. Once she got close to my face and said between clenched teeth, "It's my money." She moved away. "Anyway, the material is too slinky. It shows the size of your butt."

"Mom," said Cara, "her butt is small. Look, those are her hip bones."

"This is none of your business," Mom said to Cara. Then, turning to me, she said, "I was never that fat when I was your age. You need to go on the egg and grapefruit diet with me. Maybe you could shed those extra pounds."

"Not by Friday," I said.

"There are no extra pounds," Cara said.

Mom ignored her.

Mom finally decided on a light blue dress with puffed sleeves and a princess waist. A little border of flowers ran right under the bosom part and around the sleeves and neckline.

"I bet Nana wore this very dress when she went to her prom in 1908," I whispered to Cara, joking.

"At least it's long enough," Cara whispered back.

I gave in immediately at the shoe store. There was no use in fighting, even though my feet looked like huge black things in the closed-toe shoes Mom picked out.

In my mind, I decided to wear my summer sandals.

During dinner at Chick-Fil-A, Mom got angry. She rehashed the time she'd wasted looking for dresses.

"I spent twenty-seven damned dollars. Twenty-seven. Do you know how much material I could have gotten for that? Do you? And that dress . . . we could have gotten that piece of crap at a garage sale for a quarter."

I sat across from Mom and next to Cara. My body felt stiff, ready to get me out of the way, out of Chick-Fil-A, if necessary. I tried not to flinch as Mom slapped me with words. Cara and I ate as fast as we could.

"I didn't know to look for a dress when we were garage-saling," I said. "I didn't know I'd be going to the dance."

Cara sipped her lemonade. I swallowed half-chewed chunks of chicken. The food didn't taste good anymore. Mom ranted and raved. She kept her voice low, but sometimes it slipped over to the people sitting near. They stared at the three of us.

At last Mom got up. We were going home. I dreaded the drive back. I hated to be in the car with Mom when she was angry. It wasn't a safe place.

Though we lived only a few miles from the mall, the ride seemed to go on forever. Mom continued to complain about the dress, her voice getting angrier and angrier. I sat squished up against the window behind her. Cara sat beside me.

The two-door Escort bounced down the rocky driveway. I stared out the window, my forehead resting on the glass. Through the trees I could see flashes of Brandon's barn and greenhouse and large home. If only he hadn't asked me. If only I hadn't said yes. This was all my fault.

I held the boxed dress on my lap. My fingers touched the smoothness of the shiny cardboard. My shoes hung in a plastic bag that dangled from my wrist. They bumped against my leg. The trees on the wooded slopes pushed in on the driveway, in on us, making an umbrella of dark green, allowing only bits and pieces of the evening sun to drip through.

When she pulled into the yard, Mom shut off the engine. The car shook for a few seconds and finally died.

"Get out," Mom said. "You wasted my time tonight." She turned partway in her seat and looked back at me.

"I'm sorry," I said. I could feel Cara, tense, next to me, but I didn't dare look at her. I had to keep my eyes on Mom.

"Like hell you are."

I didn't answer. I wasn't sure if I should. I never am.

"You are so self-righteous it makes me sick," Mom said.

I had enough energy to have leapt from the car in a single bound, like Superman, if there had been a way out. But there was a problem. With both Cara and me in the backseat, who could open the front door?

"Get the hell out of this freaking car."

"Open the door," Cara said to me. Only she said it real soft.

"You," I said. I tried not to make my lips move. I slipped the bag the shoes were in from my wrist. I needed to be more free. We both watched Mom.

"Get out now." Mom's voice went up high at the end, louder and louder, so that I was surprised the glass all around us didn't shatter. I wanted to say, "Eh, what's that?" like I couldn't hear anything at all, but that would have been really dumb.

Mom started pounding on the steering wheel with the palms of both hands. "Get out, get out!" she screamed with each pound.

This was our chance. I bolted forward, leaning across Cara over the front seat, and tried to reach the door handle.

Mom hit me on the back with her fists as soon as I touched the metal. The blows knocked the breath from me and made me feel all hollow inside. But I managed to push the door open before I fell back beside Cara. She was crying.

Mom grabbed the passenger seat and threw it forward over and over again. It bounced back hard each time.

"Get the hell out of this car." Her voice was so loud I was embarrassed the neighbors would hear. That Brandon would hear.

"Let the leaves catch the sounds," I said, under my breath.

"What did you say?" Mom screamed. She turned and leaned back toward Cara and me. "What did you say?" Spit sprayed at us. "How dare you say things like that? How dare you disobey me?" Her arm stretched toward us, the fat swinging, and she slapped Cara. She grabbed me by the hair and jerked me forward.

"Hurryhurryhurry," I said to Cara. Cara tried hard to push her way between the seat and the side of the door. But Mom's weight held us trapped in the car.

Then like a miracle Cara leapt over the front seat, pulling me with her. Her fingers scratched at my arm, but I didn't care. I fell out of the car and onto the rocky driveway, landing on my knees, then rolling to one side.

Mom threw the boxes, my dress and shoes, out of the car. The dress box hit me in the head. I grabbed them both and, clutching the dress to my chest, ran with Cara.

We went to our room to hide.

CHAPTER

FIVE

When people found out that plain ol' Caitlynne Elizabeth Jackson was going to the school dance with one of the most popular guys in seventh grade, they all started staring.

I was real careful, though. I washed my hair every night that last week. And I ran a few pairs of shorts and some T-shirts through the washer so they'd be clean. I was pretty sure they weren't staring at me because I was dirty.

Comments were Oak Middle School–style. I heard things like: "She's a dog." "Why her?" "Maybe she's really nice." One girl, quite pretty, who hangs with Jennifer stopped me in the hall. She grabbed my arm. Her slender fingers were cold.

"So you sleeping with him?"

"What?" I pulled my arm free.

"You're white trash. There'd be no other reason," she said, matter-of-fact, and slung her long, light blond hair over one shoulder. She laughed a tinkling laugh and said, "Inquiring minds want to know."

"You've got something black stuck between your teeth," I said. It was a lie. But suddenly I knew that no dress I could have bought would make the girls at my school like me.

Mostly, though, kids said things in whispers. Except for Kathy.

"I cannot believe you!" she shouted across the room at me in art class.

I grinned at her and got my watercolor, then went to sit at her table.

"Why didn't you tell me Brandon asked you?" Kathy's hands worked at the modeling clay she held so it would mold easily. She wanted her last project to be a rearing stallion.

I shrugged. "I was afraid maybe it was a joke. I didn't want anybody to know. And besides, I didn't think it would get around our classes so fast." I studied my art work. Something was missing, but I couldn't quite figure out what.

"Well, it has." She nodded at a group of girls at a far table. They stared boldly at me when I glanced over at them.

Then Kathy's face got serious. "What does your mom think of this whole thing?"

I shrugged. "She bought me a dress." There were bruises on my arms from the night before and a place on my back that hurt, but I pretended there was no pain. It was easy at school to act like things were different at home.

"You're kidding!" Kathy sounded surprised.

I couldn't help grinning, even though the dress waiting at home was not what I wanted.

"That is just great," she said. And I could tell by her voice that she meant it.

"New shoes, too," I said. I leaned toward Kathy and whispered, "But I don't like them much."

Kathy's hands worked. "When I go places with Liza, well, let's just say she and I don't have the same taste. It can get pretty mean."

"Mean?" I looked at Kathy. Mean is not what I would call her mom. But lots of times things are not what people think they are.

"Not mean mean." Kathy rushed to correct herself. "We argue. That's all."

"Oh."

"What about your mom?"

I looked hard at my picture. "I don't argue much with my mom."

We sat at the table a moment, me wondering if Kathy was as okay as I had always thought.

At the end of class, Kathy stood and stretched. I looked at my unfinished picture. Girls passed our table making comments. "I can't see why he'd ask her."

Kathy smiled at me as I watched the girls leave the room. "Ain't it great having them jealous?"

I wasn't so sure.

I was glad when Friday came, because it was the last day of school. We got out early so the decorations committee could have a chance to dress up the gym.

The bus trip was hot and dusty. Cara and I bounced toward home. Every time I thought of going to the dance with Brandon, my stomach turned a flip-flop.

Toward the end of the bus ride, Brandon came over to where I was. Lots of kids turned to watch him. He was smiling. When he got close to Cara and me, he sat down in our seat.

Here it comes, I thought. Everyone is in on it except me. I looked down toward my lap.

"Can I sit with you?" he asked.

I could barely nod. "You've never asked before. I like it better when you treat me like one of the guys."

Brandon's face went red. Cara looked at me with her eyebrows pushed together. I hurried to correct what I had said.

"I didn't mean it like that. I meant, this is causing

me a lot of attention that I'm not used to." I kept my voice low. "Before, girls could stand it when I was just a baseball player. Now they're about to scratch my eyes out."

Brandon laughed, then leaned across Cara, who was in the middle, and put his mouth close to my ear.

"They're stupid," he said. Then he moved away.

Some guy at the front of the bus called out Brandon's name; then most everyone seemed to have something better to do than stare at the three of us. People in the back started to talk real loud. One kid yelled out the window. Two more tossed a football around. Jennifer and her friends huddled together, then turned to stare. Cara waved at them. Debbie and Pam, twins and friends of Cara's, motioned her to their seat, and she went up to sit with them.

I sat with Brandon. He put his arm around me. His hand touched my elbow. It was hard to relax, but I kind of liked it.

Before my bus stop, Brandon squeezed my hand. Our houses were far enough apart on the road that he didn't usually leave the bus with Cara and me. Today, though, he did. Jennifer glared hard out the window.

The hot sun mixed in with the heat of bus exhaust. We stood there on my sandy bit of driveway holding hands. We talked about what would happen that night, and I knew things were going to be okay. I could tell. After a couple of minutes, Brandon and I separated, and Cara and I started the blocklong walk down our driveway.

When we got home, Cara and I changed into our bathing suits, then ran out to the lake. Mom would be home in a couple of hours. She had told me that morning, when she apologized for the bruises, that she'd help me get ready at six.

I played long enough in the water that even the ugly blue dress on the hanger in my closet was turning into a ball gown in my mind.

CHAPTER

SIX

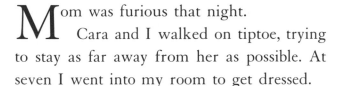

Mom was furious that night.

Cara and I walked on tiptoe, trying to stay as far away from her as possible. At seven I went into my room to get dressed.

"Stay and help me," I whispered to Cara.

"You think I'm going out there?"

I pulled the blue dress over my head. I imagined it being the shiny forest green one with a cinched waist. That dress had matched my eyes.

"No need worrying that anyone else will have the same one," Cara said.

I laughed a little. "You have a point there."

I coated mascara I'd borrowed from Kathy on my eyelashes. They felt heavy and the brush tickled and made me sneeze. Then I sat down on the bed so Cara could fix my hair. She pinned it up several different ways with a few bobby pins I had found on the floor.

We were laughing at the results when suddenly Mom was in the doorway.

"Hi," I said. Cara was partway done with my hair. Half was up, pinned to my head. The other half hung long down my back.

"Cara's doing my hair," I said stupidly. "What do you think?"

"What the hell are you getting ready for?"

Spit seemed to get thick in my mouth. I swallowed a couple of times. "There's that dance tonight." My voice came out strangled sounding.

Cara's hands rested soft on my shoulders.

"You're not going."

"But you told me I could. I told Brandon you said it was okay. He's coming to get me soon." It was hard to breathe.

"I told you the night we got that dress that you couldn't go."

"No, you didn't, Mom. I promise you didn't. If you had, I would have told Brandon at school today." I tried to breathe through my nose again.

"I hate it when you lie like this." Mom's voice was on the verge of growing loud. She still stood in the doorway, but every muscle in my body was ready.

"Well, I'm sorry," I said. "I'm really sorry." I hoped this would change her mind about my going to the dance.

Mom's hand seemed to lighten its grip on the doorway. "Where are your new shoes?"

"In the bag still," I said.

"Why don't you have them on?"

"I haven't had a chance yet. I didn't want to scuff them up, so I'm wearing these sandals till the last minute." It was a lie. I never planned to wear them. I hated the way the old-lady black shoes looked pointing out from under my dress. They seemed to be the biggest things on my body.

Mom lunged toward Cara and me. We both jumped to our feet. "Liar!" she screamed.

Cara stood on the bed, and I wondered if I could run fast enough in my dress to get away from Mom. But she was next to me in an instant, gripping my arm hard, twisting. "You're not going to the dance. I don't care what you say to me, you are not going." She shook me, and my teeth banged together.

I started crying. "I have to go. I told him I would."

"You are not going!" Mom's voice shook the window panes. She pushed me onto the bed. I fell back and my feet went up into the air, showing my dirty white sandals. Grabbing one ankle, she pulled me onto the floor.

"Don't!" Cara cried out.

There was a knock at the door. My tears stopped for a moment.

"You will not leave." Mom threatened me with her fist. "Now go tell him you can't go."

"Cara," I said, getting to my knees, then standing. "I . . . can't . . . do . . . it. . . . Will . . . you . . . please?"

Cara nodded, and started the long way around the room to the door.

I was crying so hard, I could barely take in a breath. And my darn nose wasn't working after all.

Mom punched my shoulder.

"I said for you to take care of it. Send him home."

I burst out crying again. "I'm crying too hard."

Mom pushed me forward, and I almost fell. I walked out of my bedroom, through the piled-up hall, through the filthy kitchen. The knock sounded again. "Please let him be coming to cancel," I whispered.

But he wasn't. I could tell when I opened the door. He was wearing a dark suit. There was a tiny white rosebud pinned to his lapel. He held a see-through box in his hands.

"What's wrong?" he asked.

"Nothing," I said, trying to swallow my sobs.

I touched my hair. Half was still up. I pulled out

the bobby pins. My hair fell. I smelled the lemon scent of dish soap.

Brandon held out the box to me. I could see a bit of a flower, but I didn't reach for it. "My mom changed her mind," I said. "She won't let me go."

"Why not?" His voice was soft.

I shrugged my shoulders. "I don't know."

"Come with me anyway," Brandon said, his voice almost a whisper.

A little feeling of shock went through me. "I can't do that."

"Yes, you can." Brandon stretched his hand out.

I wanted to reach for him, then run far, far away. "Good night," I said. I tried not to think about anything. I stared out far toward the old barn that was falling apart in our backyard, willing myself not to cry. "I'm sorry I ruined your evening."

I wanted to howl like a dog to get all the sadness out of me. Instead, I closed the door softly, before Brandon had even turned away.

CHAPTER

SEVEN

▼

I was still standing by the door when I heard another tap.

"Who's there?" I asked.

"It's me." I recognized Brandon's voice, but I didn't say anything. "It's Brandon Hill. Your neighbor."

"I remember who you are." I didn't open the door. Instead, I wiped at my nose and eyes with the hem of my dress. Mascara smeared there, dark. I probably looked like a strawberry. A strawberry wearing an ugly blue dress.

Then I opened the door.

Brandon stood on the bottom step. The evening sun made the grass in the yard seem very green.

"Maybe we could take a walk," he said.

"I can't." I thought I might start crying again.

Mom came thundering into the kitchen. She couldn't see Brandon because of the door. Her hand reached out for me, then stopped when she did see him. I looked at her. Her mouth made a small surprised O.

Brandon took a step closer. His face looked angry, like it had once when someone bowled into him running to third base. "Can Caity at least go walking with me? We'll stay on your property."

"Why should I care?" Mom said. She left without a word to me, pausing only to glare.

I looked at my hands.

"Let's go down by the lake," he said. "We can watch the sun set. I told my mom already that that's what we'd be doing. If you want."

I took a deep breath through my nose. I started down the steps, but I stopped partway down. Mom won't like this, I thought. I'm gonna get into more trouble.

Brandon looked up at me. He had an almost smile on his face.

I'm going anyway, I thought.

As if on cue, the faint sound of music floated over from a house across the lake. Near the water we would hear it better. Other times, I could sit quiet on the slide and hear people calling to each other all the way across the lake. For some reason sound carried better at night, too.

We walked the long way down to the shore, going past huge oak trees and around the alligator wall, past the place where Mom had had Cara and me dig a hole for the garbage, on close to the reeds where I was afraid moccasins might live.

We were on the white sand path now. A fast song echoed toward us, and from the dock came a whoop and then laughter. "I don't get why you're doing this," I said. "We've only ever been friends. Why didn't you ask one of the pretty girls at school to go?"

"I wanted to go with you."

"You never have before."

Brandon nodded.

"So why the change? Was it a dare or something? Is somebody paying you to take the second baseman out?" I felt sorry when I saw his face, sorry that I'd let go with the things I'd been thinking all week. "Lots of the girls think you're cute." My tongue was saying things I didn't really want to say.

"And what do you think?" Brandon stopped me, holding on to my arm. His hand was warm.

I shrugged. "You're my neighbor. The guy I've lived next door to since I was seven. You taught me to throw a ball. We've always been friends. But not this kind." I held my hands out, palm up. In the light they looked almost golden.

It was a quiet moment, except for the party going on across the lake.

"And you don't think anything else?"

I stopped on the path. A breeze puffed past us, moving my hair. Brandon turned to me and pushed the rest back over one shoulder.

"Caity, for a long time you were just one of the people I played ball with. Awhile back I looked at you and thought, 'Wow!'"

"Wow?" I asked. Mr. Cannon would say *wow* was not a very descriptive word. But for me, it was perfect. I kept repeating it in my mind.

Brandon took my hand and we started walking again, to the two frayed lawn chairs that sat at the edge of the lake. The water licked at the shore with a tiny *lip, lip* sound. A breeze moved toward us, pushing mosquitoes ahead of it. The sun sank lower.

Brandon and I sat down. Underneath me the chair squeaked, and I crossed my fingers, hoping it wouldn't throw me the way it sometimes did if I wasn't careful. Slowly I let my leg muscles relax. The chair held sure.

"So why wouldn't your mom let you go tonight?" Brandon dragged his lawn chair close to mine, then settled back, resting his arms and legs like he was going to get a tan.

"She was mad."

"I could see that." He was quiet a minute. Then he said, "I heard her yelling."

My face colored immediately. "Yelling?" The word came out garbled, almost like it wasn't a word.

"Yeah. I hear her lots. My dad worries about it. My mom says it's none of our business what happens over here."

"You've all heard her?" My stomach felt queasy.

"Yeah. It makes me sad for you. Why do you let her yell at you so much?"

"What kind of question is that? I don't *let* her. She just does it." I thought for a moment I might cry. Instead, I squinted at the setting sun. Everything near us looked like it was painted over with a light orange wash. Even the lake had a glazed orange color to it.

I glanced squint-eyed over at Brandon.

He was looking at me. "Don't be mad. I just wondered."

"I'd rather not talk about it," I said, and I looked out over the lake. Across the sky a full moon chased the sun. We were quiet. I sat uncomfortable in my chair, my dress suddenly itching at all the seams.

"I watch you and Cara swim sometimes," Brandon said after a bit. "You like swimming at night, don't you?"

I tried to make my voice sound normal, even though the blood pounding in my ears made it hard for me to hear my own self. "Oh yeah. You don't. Ever. Swim in the lake, I mean. How come?"

"My mom is worried about snakes. And there's an alligator out there. Besides, we have our pool."

"Yes," I said, feeling silly.

The sun settled down, pulling the light blue sky with it, like it was covering up with a pale-colored sheet. The moon brought out a deeper-colored blanket of sky which darkened the higher it climbed.

A song with a fast beat thumped across the lake. Brandon sang off-key with the music. I settled down, trying to pretend he hadn't said anything about Mom.

"Isn't this a great song?" he asked. He snapped his fingers. I hoped he wouldn't get up and start dancing alone under the darkening sky, where bits of light were just beginning to flicker. We sat out at the lake for a long time and talked about school and the coming summer. I breathed in deep the warm night air. It pushed away all my embarrassment.

I'll remember this night forever, I thought. I'll remember the moon and stars and breeze. And even this dress.

"I've got to go," Brandon said. He looked at his watch. "It's after eleven."

My stomach flopped. Did Mom care how late it was? I looked toward my house. No lights were on, only a soft glow that came from the room I shared with Cara. I knew she was reading.

Brandon walked me to the door. I climbed the steps and he followed me. "Don't forget this," he said, handing me the boxed flower.

"Yeah. Okay. Thanks." I took the flower.

Brandon leaned forward then, to kiss me. I turned my head at the last second and his lips landed on my ear. The smack echoed. He jumped down the stairs and disappeared into the night.

"See ya," he called.

I tiptoed inside the dark house. In the kitchen, I took the flower from the box and pinned it into my hair with a loose bobby pin. I felt my way along the hall, running my fingers along the cypress walls until I was in the room I shared with Cara. She was asleep. I turned off her reading light, then pulled my dress off and threw it over a chair. I kicked my sandals away from my feet, and, in my underwear, I danced alone in the ghostly light of my room.

"Go to sleep," Mom growled from the doorway. Her voice made me jump. Quickly I found a long T-shirt and climbed into bed. I left the flower in my hair.

CHAPTER

EIGHT

▼

All the next day, Mom was mad. Cara and I stayed out of her way. I wore the rose in my hair until Mom finally came up and snatched it out. She threw it on the floor and smashed it with her bare heel, twisting her foot a few times. I didn't say anything. But when she walked away, I picked up the crushed flower and pinned it back near my ear. Rose smell was thick in the air, a soft cloud of perfume by my head.

In bits and pieces I told Cara what had happened with Brandon. I kept some things private, like the way I felt when I thought of him saying "Wow!"

In the afternoon, when Cara and I were down at the lake, Brandon called over to us.

"We're playing ball later. You two want to play?"
I looked at Cara. She nodded.

"Sure," I yelled back.

We made ourselves a big lunch, turkey sandwiches with thick-sliced tomatoes, chips and lime Kool-Aid. That morning, after sitting for a long time at the computer and not writing, Mom had gone out to the car. She had driven away and come back later with bags of food. Now the cabinets seemed to burst with delicious things to eat. It was strange that Mom would do something like this. She never went shopping. Mostly she would buy things here and there, as the mood struck her. But I didn't complain and neither did Cara.

At three o'clock, Cara and I went to the acre lot to meet with the neighborhood guys. Jennifer, Mandy and Elaine showed up too. They came over to where I was warming up, throwing a ball back and forth with Cara.

"I didn't see you and Brandon at the dance," Jennifer said when she got up close to me.

"We didn't go," I said. The sun was high and hot. Sweat trickled down my forehead. Jennifer and her friends stood near, looking very cool.

"I told you," said Mandy. "They *were* making out."

"Did you two go all the way?" Elaine asked.

My heart was pounding hard. I felt so embarrassed

I couldn't even work up a good spit. "Leave me alone." I threw the ball hard to Cara.

"You can tell us," said Mandy.

I moved away and went to stand on second base. Brandon came running over from his house, and the three girls hurried to meet him.

"We're the cheerleaders," Jennifer said to Brandon, sliding up next to him and smiling into his face. She whispered something and Brandon looked over at me. Had she asked him the same awful question?

He waved at me and the game began.

I played against Brandon's team, with Cara and five other guys. There weren't enough people to make complete teams, what with vacations starting and families being gone, so we rotated in for batting.

Brandon hit a good ball that sent him to second. I stood a few feet off the plate, knowing in a different way that he was near. My face turned pink at the thought of him kissing my ear the night before. I looked over at the sidelines. Jennifer stood with her hands on her hips, watching us.

"You gonna let me steal?" Brandon asked, his voice teasing.

"No way," I said. The sun was hot, and I wondered how I looked. Not as good as Jennifer, but better than I had last night. "I'll put your old self right out if you take a step offa that base."

Brandon laughed.

I glanced at him. The sun was bright in his hair, making it look not so brown.

"Kiss her and get it over with, Hill," somebody yelled at home plate. "We wanna play the game and the two of you are holding us up."

"Well, thank you for permission," Brandon said. He stepped off the base and came over to me.

"Caity," he said, reaching out. He took my hand in one of his and my mitt in his other hand. He pulled the mitt, with me still attached, close to his chest. I had never noticed how white his teeth were before. I had never noticed that they were a little crooked.

Brandon leaned forward and kissed my face. The guys and Cara started whooping. He turned and bowed, sweeping one hand against the dried-out grass of the playing field.

"We're ready," Brandon said, moving back to second base.

My face felt like it was a red light. I got back into position like nothing out of the ordinary had happened.

Somebody smacked the ball high and to the left and Brandon was gone. Running to third and then home. Jennifer hurried to him when he came in at the base. I watched them out of the corner of my eye. She clapped him on the back and tried to hug him, but Brandon moved away.

"Action Jackson," he called to me. Jennifer and her friends didn't do much cheering after that. They left early.

A couple of hours later the game drifted apart.

Mom never called us in.

"Boy, is she mad," I said to Cara. We were sitting down at the shoreline letting minnows, tiny and silver, nibble at our toes. The water made my feet look pale.

"Yeah, I guess so." Cara didn't seem too worried.

There was an uneasy feeling in the pit of my stomach. "What's she doing?"

"Writing on that novel."

I nodded. Mom spent a lot of time writing.

"A whole, wide summer," Cara said. She lay back on the sand, stretching her arms wide. She flipped droplets of water toward the center of the lake. They sailed through the air looking like daytime lightning bugs.

"Yep." I nodded at the sky. It was clear blue. The sun moved quickly toward the west.

"Think she'll ignore us long this time?" I asked.

"If we're lucky."

"I hate it when things are like this."

"She's always mad. And I don't mind if all she does is not talk. It doesn't hurt."

"It bugs me," I said. "When I ask her a question, she won't answer."

"You'd rather she answer with a slap and a holler?" Cara asked.

I laughed. "No, I'd rather she be nice."

But Mom wasn't. If we got near her that evening, she'd say, "Get out of my sight. You both make me sick."

The sun settled down to rest and Mom went swimming. I peeked on her desk and saw a letter to the electric company saying she was going to pay for three months in advance. I wondered where she had moved her computer. I felt guilty for looking at Mom's private stuff. She didn't like it if I read her book unless she told me to. Of course, this *wasn't* her book, but she'd probably be angry about my reading it.

I looked out the window, spying almost, so she wouldn't see me. Cara went to bed to read. Still Mom swam. I remembered my sister's dream and worried. When it got too dark to see really good, I sat out on the screened-in porch and listened for Mom's splashes. I wondered. Could I run from the house, to the lake, swim to where she was, and get her to shore if she was drowning? When she finally pulled herself from the water, I ran into the house and plopped into a chair to make it look like I hadn't been nervous. I waited for her to come inside.

Mom's body was shiny and wet. Her black hair dripped. I could tell by her walk she was still mad. But at least I'd be able to go to bed now.

I closed the book I had pretended to read and stood up, stretching tall toward the ceiling.

"I saw you watching me," she said. "You're a sick girl to watch your own mother."

"I was afraid something might happen to you," I said. "I watched to make sure everything was okay."

"Caity, you need psychiatric help." Mom moved past me, large, leaving trails of water on the wooden floor. "I can't stay in a house full of sicko children. I've got to get out. I'm leaving."

"Are you going to McDonald's?" I asked. Sometimes Mom does that, leaves at night to get something to eat from a place that stays open late.

Mom looked disgusted. "You are so stupid. I am leaving for good." She said the last words slow, one-at-a-time slow, right in my face. I could smell onions on her breath.

"What do you mean?" I had heard what she'd said, but I was afraid, and fear made it hard for me to understand.

Mom smiled. She looked off over my head so intensely that I turned to see what she was staring at.

There was nothing behind me but the wall and a pile of dirty clothes.

"School's out for the summer. I'm going to Tifton. I'm going to write the book I've always wanted to write." Writing a blockbuster best-seller is something

Mom talks about. When she's happy she tells me she wants me to do the cover illustration. And Tifton is where our family comes from. My great-grandfather lived there when he was a little boy.

I had to breathe through my mouth to get any air. "When are you going?"

"Now. I've taken care of everything. Paid the bills for the summer. The rent. The gas and electricity. I didn't worry about the phone. You won't need the phone."

"Are you going in that?" I asked, pointing to Mom's bathing suit. It was a joke.

She slapped me hard across the face. She was so fast I didn't even have time to duck. Mom pounded from the living room toward her bedroom. I stood dazed a moment, then followed.

"I'll wake up Cara," I said. "We can be ready in a few minutes." My face was stinging. I stood back a bit so I'd have a chance to get out of the way if she tried to hit me again.

"You're not going," Mom said. She had gotten out an old suitcase. It rested openmouthed on the bed.

"Huh?" I said. Only it wasn't a question. It was more like a garbled word. "What?"

"I'm going alone." Mom went to her closet and started throwing dresses into the suitcase.

I suddenly felt very afraid. "We'll be good," I said.

My voice was a loud whisper. "I promise. We'll be real careful not to bother you."

Mom was digging through her drawers now, throwing out underwear and a couple of bras. They landed in a white pile on top of the dresses.

I ran to her side.

"It's all taken care of," Mom said.

"Have you talked to Nana?" I asked. "Is she coming to stay with us?"

"Oh, puh-lease. She wouldn't watch the two of you even if I paid her. She likes you less than I do. And she never does anything to help me out. Never." Mom suddenly sounded like she was going to cry.

"Yes she does," I said. "She made you all your clothes."

Mom ignored me.

"She always cooks the meals at Thanksgiving and Christmastime. She loves us."

"She doesn't love me. Not the way she loves Margaret." Aunt Margaret is Mom's only sister. "Or Ryan. She really loves Ryan. Because he's a lawyer and keeps her living in style."

Uncle Ryan *is* a lawyer, but he doesn't do that much for Nana. She has her house and a pension from when my granddaddy died. I know these things because I've listened in at Christmas when the grown-ups sit around the dining room table and talk about money. Nana never wants any.

"She loves you, Mom." I ran to her side. Her voice was making a big bubble of sadness rise to the surface of my throat. The pain crackled right behind my tongue. "And I love you, too."

Mom pushed me away. I fell backward over garbage that had been swept into a pile.

"You are not going." Mom's voice was as big as the room. It filled up the corners and pushed at the walls. She came toward me and I scooted back fast. But she ignored me and just reached for dry clothes.

"Listen," I said from the floor. "Listen. We'll be good. I promise. I won't bother you and neither will Cara. We'll be real quiet while you're writing. And I'll edit for you." Mom always had me check her writing to see if it made sense. "I'll buy your cigarettes. You won't even have to get up from your writing." It was then that I saw she had already packed her computer away. It waited in the big white Packard Bell box, taped securely with masking tape.

I stood. Mom continued to pack, placing her manuscript, hundreds of pages' worth, on top of her clothes.

"Don't leave us, Mom. It gets scary at night." I edged over to where she stood looking down at her book. "Don't go."

Mom slapped the suitcase shut. She laughed a funny laugh, then took some dry clothes and headed off to the bathroom. I ran after her, taking tiny steps, wanting to grab her around the belly and stop her from going. I reached to touch her and she elbowed me away.

Suddenly I was crying. I ran up beside her, bumping into the hall wall because there wasn't room for the two of us side by side.

"Maybe I can get a part-time job," I said. "I'm good at cleaning. Maybe I could be a maid."

Mom closed the bathroom door in my face. I leaned my head on the jamb. I was really scared now. And really crying.

"I'm sorry I was so bad," I said. "I swear I'll do better. Please don't go."

But Mom didn't answer. She came out of the bathroom, went into her bedroom and got her boxed computer and carried it out to the car. I ran along behind, begging her not to leave. She stomped back to the house, pushing me away whenever I got too close, and grabbed up her suitcase. One of the buckles popped open and the suitcase sagged on one side, showing its guts of clothes and papers, but Mom ignored it. Instead of stopping and closing it again, she clutched one arm around it.

"Let me help," I said. I tried to take her clothes from her, but Mom wouldn't let me. She got the keys and went outside.

"There's some spending money in the honey jar," she said. Her voice was icy.

"Mom, I'll do better. I'll keep the house Sparkle City for you."

We were outside now, nearing the small blue car. The passenger door was open and the light inside glowed, showing the words *Packard Bell* dark on the white box.

Mom threw the suitcase onto the backseat.

"I'll make breakfast, lunch and dinner and let you sleep late."

She climbed in.

I tried to hold the door open.

The engine started.

"Don't go," I said. "Please don't go."

Mom pushed the door hard into me, smacking my hands and one knee, shaking me loose. Then she pulled the door shut and put the car in gear. She pulled around me and I ran after her, barefoot up the driveway, a few yards. I noticed one of the taillights was out. The other burned red, growing smaller and smaller in the night until it was gone.

I sat down in the dirt and rocks of the driveway.

I sat and waited.

I listened for the car to come back, listened for its familiar cough.

The ground was warm. The air was warm. I was warm.

Mosquitoes began to bite.

I rested my head on my knees and waited awhile longer.

Then, in slow motion, I got up. I felt so tired. I wondered how late it was. I started for the house. All the lights burned bright, making long yellow boxes on the ground.

We need curtains, I thought.

I went inside to my room. I crawled into bed, not even bothering to get undressed. After a while, I got out of bed and went over to Cara. She was sleeping on her side. I crawled in next to her and she said something about riding a three-legged dog. I would have laughed if it had been any other night.

It took me a long time to go to sleep because when I closed my eyes, the memory of the one taillight glowed, like a red eye, in my mind.

CHAPTER

NINE

▼

"**M**om's gone."

It was the first thing I thought when I woke up. I said it so soft that my lips smacked together with the sound of it. I opened my eyes halfway. The sun was patterned on the ceiling, long bright strips. Oak leaves jigsawed the light.

"What are you doing in my bed?" Cara asked.

"Mom left last night," I said straight out.

Cara didn't say anything.

"She went to Georgia. To finish her book."

"I know."

I leaned upon my elbow and looked at my sister. "How?"

"I heard you two last night."

I was embarrassed that Cara had heard

me begging our mother not to leave us. And mad, too.

"Why didn't you get up and come and try and stop her?" I asked.

"I didn't want to," Cara said. Her voice was flat. "I'm glad she's gone."

I didn't say anything. Did Cara mean what she said?

"Well, she'll be back soon, I bet," I said.

"I hope not." Cara got up and started getting dressed.

I lay in bed a minute longer, thinking.

"It's summer," said Cara. She was looking at me in the mirror. "What are we gonna do?"

"Well." I bit at my chewed nails. One hurt because I had pulled it down into the quick. A thin line of blood showed at the edge. "I'm figuring Mom has gone off to scare us. I think she'll be back before we know it. She's never done anything like this before. So, I guess the thing to do is wait."

"No," Cara said.

"No, what?"

"I mean, no. I'm not talking about Mom at all. I'm talking about us enjoying the summer. What fun are we going to have? I'm gonna call Pam and Debbie over right now." Cara had been brushing her hair with her fingers. Now she stopped and headed out the door to call the twins.

"Wait," I said, jumping up out of bed. Luckily I was already dressed. "We need to talk."

"I'm gonna talk. I'm gonna talk to my friends."

"No, Cara. I'm serious." I took hold of Cara's arm and she turned to look at me. "Don't tell them Mom is gone . . . that she left, I mean."

"Why not?" I could tell by the way she was moving around that Cara was antsy to get to the phone.

"Think about it," I said. "If somebody finds out and Mom never comes back, they might separate us. You know, put us in different houses to live. I've read about stuff like that happening."

Cara eyed me. "Okay, I won't tell them anything."

"And I think we should try and straighten up."

Cara groaned. "Why that? I don't wanna."

"I don't either," I said. "But what would Debbie and Pam say about our place? Remember that one time you stayed overnight with them? You said everything was nice and neat." Really I didn't care if Pam and Debbie saw the house messy. I wanted to get things done in case Mom came back. "We could work for a while and then have them come over and play. I'll call Kathy, too."

"Only for a little while," Cara said. "Then play."

"Deal," I said.

We ate breakfast, then began to work. It was hard, but we managed to get the front room cleaned and the bathroom. Even the kitchen, and that was the worst.

"Aren't you scared?" I asked Cara while scrubbing the pots. My hands had turned white and wrinkled, I'd had them in the water for so long. "Aren't you afraid about what's going to happen to us?"

Cara looked at me from where she was wiping down the outside of the fridge. She shrugged. "What could be worse than what has already happened?" She gazed at me a long moment. Her eyes were big and sad.

"Us not being together," I said, and I turned back to the sink and started scrubbing a small saucepan.

Pam and Debbie came over to see Cara after lunch. The twins weren't allowed to swim because there were no adults, so the three of them played Monopoly and listened to the radio really loud.

I called Kathy.

"Hey," I said when she got on the phone.

"Caity, what are you doing?"

"Calling to see if you want to come over."

Kathy was quiet. "I better not. I have so much to do. I'm off to Jerry's place in a couple of days."

"My mom's not here," I said.

"She isn't?"

"No."

Kathy took a big breath, then whispered into the

65

phone, "Caity, I know you're gonna think this is dumb, but she'll probably come back while I'm there. I'm scared of her."

Now it was my turn to not say anything. At last I cleared my throat. "Why are you scared of her?" My voice was low, even though I could hear my sister and her friends outside still playing.

"This one time, the last time when I spent the night with you?"

"Yeah," I said. It had been on a Friday night more than six months before.

"You went to talk to your mom about coming to my house for Saturday night. Do you remember?"

"I remember she wouldn't let me." My face began to color.

"I heard her talking to you, Caity. It was real mean. So I started down the hall to tell you to forget it. And, when I got there, she was hitting you with her fist."

I didn't say anything. I was glad Kathy couldn't see how embarrassed I was.

"With her fist, Caity. In the back. And once on the side of your head. It scared me. I . . . I don't like her. I don't want to come over."

"I understand," I said. "I guess I'd be afraid, too." Maybe. "Call me when you get back from Georgia."

"I promise." Kathy sounded relieved.

We talked for a few more minutes, then hung up. I looked out at Cara, playing in a patch of shade with her friends. When was the last time she had invited anyone over? It seemed long ago. Was Cara afraid?

That night, after Pam and Debbie went home, I talked with Cara again about things to worry over. It was dark. The radio played. Cara was getting ready for bed. She had a couple of books to read. I was nervous. For some reason nighttime is always scarier.

"Think of all the things that could happen to us," I said. "I want to call someone, maybe Nana, and tell her we're alone."

"Not me," said Cara. "You know how Mom feels about Nana. Mom said she doesn't like us. I don't want to go where we're not liked."

"Nana likes us. Maybe not as much as she likes some of the other grandchildren, but I know she likes us."

"And we don't know her that well," Cara said.

"We know her better than any foster care people."

"Yeah, but I'd feel funny going and staying with her."

There wasn't a lot for me to say. Mom *had* said that stuff about Nana. And I believed it even though Nana always treated us well when we visited her. Which really wasn't that often. Especially lately. Mom always seemed angry at Nana about something or other.

"Anyway, I wanna try it alone," said Cara. "I think we'll be okay."

"We could drown," I said, joking.

"We both swim too good for that."

"A fire might start."

"It's summer. We won't cook unless we need to. And we won't use the fireplace."

"A hurricane."

"Those happen in the late summer or fall."

"A killer might come tapping at the windows."

Cara looked at me. I wondered if she remembered all the times Mom had snuck out of the house at night and gone around near the windows making noises like she was something trying to get in. "We'll sleep together and leave a few of the lights on. No one will bother us. We live pretty far away from people. I think we'll be safe."

Cara was right. No one did bother us.

And I was wrong. Mom didn't come back.

She didn't call. She didn't send money. She didn't do anything.

We played hard all day, every day. We did our best to keep things straightened. The house wasn't always clean, but I wouldn't have been embarrassed if Kathy had wanted to come over. Everything seemed to change because Mom was gone. Cara and I were happy. Sometimes I wondered what Mom was doing. At lunch, was she eating at Burger King? Was she spending all her time typing at her computer? Was the book coming along good? Did she miss us?

That's what I wondered most of all. Did she miss us?

Because I missed her, in a strange way. I missed the few times she was nice. I missed her reading her novel to Cara and me.

After two weeks I stopped listening for Mom to pull in the driveway. Cara and I made sure we were good and tired when it was time for sleep. We moved into Mom's room because her bed was bigger and we had more space. And if I couldn't sleep, I would sometimes wake up my sister and we would go skinny-dipping, with only the moon and stars and a few lightning bugs and frogs to see us.

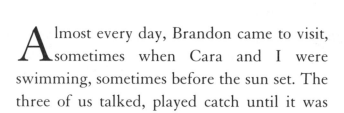

CHAPTER

TEN

Almost every day, Brandon came to visit, sometimes when Cara and I were swimming, sometimes before the sun set. The three of us talked, played catch until it was too dark to see or went places together on our bikes.

One afternoon Brandon came over after lunch, and we decided to get a game together. While Cara made calls to the different players, Brandon and I sat out on the alligator wall and waited.

He sat close, smelling like being outside. The sunlight played on us both, pushing through the oak leaves, dropping patterns on our arms and legs.

"Caity," Brandon asked, "where's your mom?"

I looked up from the long piece of grass I was tearing into tiny pieces. I was so surprised by the question I wondered if I had given myself whiplash, I jerked my head up so hard.

"What do you mean?" I asked.

He smiled at me. "It's been quiet over here. And her car's gone every time I come over. Even at night the car is gone."

Something like panic began to rise in my throat. It was kind of like the fear I felt when Mom would start hollering.

"Uh," was all I could say. I swallowed a couple of times. Behind us, I heard the screen door slam shut with a wooden clap. Cara called out, "Everybody can come."

Brandon looked back at her. He was no longer smiling, but his face was . . . well, it wasn't mean or mad or angry. Just curious. "Good. How long before they get here?"

"Probably a half hour or so." Cara plopped down near my feet. She leaned her head back a little and her blondish brown hair spread out over the green grass.

What a pretty picture, I thought. But it was like I was all numb inside, except for my eyes. It was like I was seeing her hair very yellow and the grass very green, and it didn't really matter if I could talk or not because the colors were so bright.

"What's wrong?" Cara asked, once she looked at me.

Were my eyes bulging or something? "Nothing." I shook my head.

"I asked Caity where your mom has gone to. She's never here anymore," Brandon said.

"Oh, she left a long time ago," Cara said with a shrug of her shoulders. "Went off to write a book or some such crap."

"Cara," I said, my mouth finally working.

"You can trust Brandon," Cara said. "I'd think you'd know that by now."

"Well, I do." I stumbled for words.

Brandon smiled again. "I wondered what happened. Even my parents have noticed that things are different over here. At first, they thought you all were on vacation, but they're always seeing you swimming."

"Please don't tell them she's gone," I said. "If a grown-up found out, they'd tell somebody. Maybe send Cara and me to different places. We don't want to leave each other." Suddenly leaving the lake meant much more than just being separated from Cara, even though that was the most important part. "I don't want either of us to leave here."

"Neither do I," Brandon said. Then he leaned close, closing his eyes, and rested his head on mine. I closed my eyes, too.

"Don't do anything gross," Cara said.

Brandon put his arm around me. His hand patted my shoulder. I sat very still, and for a moment I thought I'd cry. I couldn't help thinking what it would have been like if Mom had ever held me like this. Like she loved me.

We made Brandon swear he'd never tell anyone that Mom was gone. Then we told him everything that had happened. He nodded a lot and asked a few questions and even said he'd sneak us food if we needed it.

"But my family's leaving the last of July," he said. "What will happen to you then?"

"We'll be fine," I said. "We don't need anything now. Mom bought food before she left. And I'm sure she'll be back before long."

"No she won't," said Cara.

"Maybe," I said.

That day, when the game was over and long after the sun had set, Cara and I went down to the water.

Mosquitoes hummed high-pitched songs in my ears. I fanned them away with my hand. The moon was moving high in the sky, close to being almost exactly over the middle of the lake. There was a round yellow moon in the water, which rippled with breezes. The disk in the sky didn't seem to move at all.

A few lights were on at Brandon's house. There was a party going on. I perched on the slide and wondered who had been invited. The music that came across the water was old sounding, but I recognized a little of it from movies I had seen.

I saw somebody walk down to the shore of the Hills' property. I couldn't tell who it was. A long shadow spread before the person. And then he called to me.

"Caity, is that you?" It was Brandon. His voice carried over to me softlike.

"Yes," I said. "Cara and I are out swimming tonight."

"Can I come over?" he asked. Without waiting for me to answer, he started walking through the baseball field and the wild grasses that separated our homes.

Cara stood near the slide, her toes touching the water.

"You gonna let him kiss you?" she asked.

"Maybe," I said.

"Gross."

I smiled at my little sister, feeling, suddenly, much older than her. "We'll probably do it like the movie stars do."

"Double gross." Cara splashed into the water, and when she was waist high in it, she dove under. After a few seconds her head broke the surface. She smoothed her hair off her forehead, then lay back and floated, her arms stretched out to either side of her body, like a shiny T.

I looked over to where Brandon pushed toward me. He whistled something I had heard from the piano at his house. He was wearing shorts and a breezy shirt that rippled all around him.

Seeing him, getting closer, made a bubble pop in my stomach. Was this what having a boyfriend was like? Feeling happy, feeling older, bubbles popping in my guts all the time?

Brandon was on our property now. After a few moments he stood near the slide. But when he stepped toward me, I slid down into the water. It closed warm over my head, and for a little bit all I heard was the pounding of my own blood. I swam toward the springs and the water cooled. Then I turned at the thought of something other than water coming out from the holes and swam up.

"Come out here with me," Brandon said.

Cara was swimming to shore. I swam through the silk-soft water, too. I beat Cara to the shallows and went to where Brandon stood.

We walked, holding hands, until my bathing suit was dry. Then we sat on one lawn chair, watching Cara swim, white and ghostlike. We talked about the day and my mom and each other until, finally, Brandon's older brother called to him to come home. And Cara and I went into the house, which wasn't seeming as lonely as before.

CHAPTER

ELEVEN

For some reason, having Brandon know that Cara and I lived all alone made it easier. If I wanted, I could call him up and talk to him when I felt scared. I knew that when we ran out of food and money, if Mom still wasn't back, and Cara was sure she wouldn't be, we could get something to eat from him. I didn't know if I could beg food off of Brandon, but I thought if I ever had to, he was there.

Kathy never wrote. I hadn't really expected her to because Jerry always keeps Kathy and her younger brother busy when they're together. But sometimes I thought of letters in my head to send to her.

Dear Kathy—

You wouldn't believe the sunsets lately. They are so full of color. I can see one of your stallions riding in front of the sky.

Or

Dear Kathy—

Things have been very calm here, now that Mom is gone. I think you would have fun if you stayed overnight. Sorry it was bad for you that one time you came.

Or

Dear Kathy—

I wish I knew my father better and could spend some time with him. Or even Cara's dad. Maybe things wouldn't be so bad knowing two people cared about me, even if they didn't live with me anymore.

The only bill that came was the phone bill. Mom was true to her word and didn't pay in advance for it. We got two late notices before someone came and shut it off. I kept the envelopes, stamped in red ink OVERDUE, on the coquina mantel of our fireplace.

"They'll put her in jail, don't you think?" I asked Cara one afternoon. We were floating on the lake in an old metal boat we had pulled out of the garage. We'd filled small holes up thick with hot glue. The glue seemed to hold, which I felt really glad about because we were far across the lake now, where the alligator supposedly lived. I didn't want to take a chance on sinking. It made my stomach quiver to think about the boat filling up with water.

We rowed with mismatched oars that we'd taken from the wall of the garage. Every once in a while we'd paddle with a lot of energy, then float to a stop and just bob along in the water.

"Put who in jail?" asked Cara. She was lying back in the boat, her hair over the edge and floating in the water. Every so often a fish would swim to the surface and try to take a bite of the strands, which were gold-like on the lake.

"Mom. She's been gone awhile now." I was drawing. I didn't stop while I talked, just sketched, looking out at the reeds, growing tall, slender and green.

"Not long enough for me."

I ignored her answer. "Remember hearing about those kids whose mom and dad were gone for a week on vacation? Remember that the police were waiting for them at the airport when they got back from wherever it was they had gone?"

Cara opened one eye slightly. "Maybe she's not coming back. Maybe we'll never see her again."

"Doesn't that scare you?"

"No."

"Scares the hell outta me, 'scuse my French."

"Why?" Cara sat up. "Let's paddle out of these weeds. There might be water moccasins in them."

I put my paddle hard into the water and we rowed away from the edge. We were drifting closer to the high grass that grew thick on this side of the lake. No one lived over here.

I felt a little irritated that I had let us float so far. I'd gotten caught up in my drawing. My pad of paper and sketch pencils were on the seat beside me. If I had paid attention instead of trying to draw the water scene in front of me . . .

I didn't want to get too close to a nest of moccasins. They would attack, I knew that. I'd seen it on a television show.

I shivered at the thought, goose bumps rising on my arms despite the hot sun.

Relax and paddle, I thought. Get on back to the other side of the lake. I could do the rest of the drawing from memory.

After a few minutes of paddling, Cara and I slowed down. I checked behind us. No snakes followed in our wake. Still I knew I'd feel better moving on home.

We paddled across the lake, the sun high overhead. Tiny waves of water slapped against the metal of the boat, making a peaceful sound. Cara and I talked.

"Don't worry about being alone," my sister said. "I tell you, things are gonna be okay. I feel it in my gut. And besides, we're together."

"What if Mom stops paying for things? Just lets them go so bill collectors shut everything off?"

"You worry too much."

"You don't worry enough." I was struck with how dumb what I had said was. Cara was only eleven years old. A kid. And I was asking her to help me worry about money. That was my job. "I don't mean that," I said. "You don't need to worry."

I looked back at her and she smiled at me, her teeth showing up very white because her skin was so tan.

"Don't you worry either," she said.

CHAPTER

TWELVE

▼

"How much?" Cara asked.

"Forty-three dollars," I said. We were standing at the kitchen table, the honey jar between us. I held the wrinkled dollar bills in my hand.

"Not too much."

"Well, lucky for us Mom did all that shopping before she left."

"She was planning on leaving then. That's why she got the food, you know."

I nodded and stuck the money back into the brown and beige jar shaped like the bottom half of a bear. The lid, a bear head with a bee buzzing near, had gotten broken a long time before. "I'm glad she planned," I said. "Or we would have had to dig into this before now."

The cupboards were empty. The freezer food was gone. The fridge was bare except the bottoms and sides. They were splashed with stuff that had spilled and dried fast. Or bled through the packages.

"So let's ride our bikes up to Wilkens', " Cara said. "That's only a few miles away."

"No. Things cost too much there," I said. "If we ride on out to Piggly Wiggly, we'll get better prices."

"How do we carry the groceries home?"

"We'll only get a few things. And we'll wear our backpacks."

"Well, let's get going," said Cara. "I'm starving."

We had finished up the last of the pot pies for lunch that afternoon. It was seven in the evening and my stomach was beginning to growl.

I took the money back out of the jar and put it into my pocket. It made a small knot there. I hated to use it. This was all we had left until Mom came home. If she came home. But there was nothing else we could do. And what if Mom came home and got mad because we had spent the money? There was so much to worry about. I tried to shrug off the way I felt. We shouldered our packs, got our bikes and set off.

The ride to Piggly Wiggly was hot. The only breeze came from cars driving past us on the road. I was glad for that, even though the air that swirled around us stunk.

By the time we got to the store, sweat was running

down my face, running down my back and making my bra wet. It was a gross feeling. Nothing like swimming with my clothes on. We parked our bikes. Cara was as red-faced as I looked in the reflection of the door that swung open with a *swoosh* to let us in to shop. The store air was cool. I stood still, sniffing the smells that I knew meant we would eat tonight. The aroma of barbecued ribs filled the air. I was so hungry I felt like I could have eaten the welcome sign.

"Don't get a cart," I said, fingering the ball of money in my pocket. "Let's get one of those red baskets. That way we can carry what we get home."

"Good thinking," Cara said, and winked at me. I could see she was glad to be here, too.

We walked up and down the aisles looking for food. The floors were polished so glossy that I could see myself in them. The air was cool and fresh smelling. It breezed past my underarms, feeling good but reminding me the next time I pedaled all the way to Piggly Wiggly I needed to wear deodorant.

"What do we want?" Cara asked. She was looking down the candy aisle. The chocolate smell there was so strong that I almost couldn't smell my armpits. I pushed Cara past the aisle. My stomach growled.

"Whatever we get we have to be careful," I said. "There's not much money and I think you're right about Mom not coming home too soon."

Cara rolled her eyes at me. "At all, you mean."

I ignored her. "There is still a chance she'll come back. I don't want to get in trouble for buying the wrong thing."

Cara rolled her eyes again. Higher this time.

"Hope those don't fall out," I said. "Let's spend ten dollars a week."

We were standing in the frozen food section. One of the freezers kicked on and started buzzing. A little lady in a purple dress opened the glass door and pulled out a half gallon of Rocky Road ice cream. Cold air puffed out at us. When she shut the door, the glass fogged.

"Ten dollars isn't very much," Cara said. "That ice cream she bought was two forty-nine."

"I know. But look. Things that are premade always cost more. Like those pizza pocket things. They're more than three dollars. A buck apiece. If we think things through and are careful, our money will go further."

"I don't care what we buy," Cara said. "Let's just hurry."

In the end we got a package of rice and two cans of chili, four bananas and four apples. A ten-pound bag of potatoes, and oil to cook them in. We also got flour tortillas, two packages, and strawberry yogurt that was four for a dollar. We got a really cheap loaf of bread. Last of all, we picked out a half gallon of milk.

With tax, the total came to eleven dollars and thirty-six cents. I was pretty proud we had done it. But it scared me that we had run over.

While we were filling our backpacks in front of the store, we slurped yogurt from the containers. My stomach still felt tight, but at least I wasn't so shaky.

Riding home that night, I tried to think things through. "We need to get jobs," I said.

We pulled onto Markham Road, the street that ran in front of our driveway. There were two more miles to go before we could eat. I planned to make a huge pot of rice and pour a can of chili on top.

Cara looked at me sideways. "Doing what?"

I shrugged. "I'm not sure. Something we can make some money from."

"We've got money."

"Not enough to keep us alive for long." My back was aching from the food. I had taken the heavier things so Cara wouldn't have to carry them.

"So now you're thinking Mom'll never come home?" Cara's voice was even. "Before you thought she'd be back at any minute. Why'd you change your mind?"

"For all we know, Cara, Mom's sitting down there right now. We've been gone awhile. She could have come home."

I thought of how I'd feel to see the car in the driveway, parked under one of the big oaks. The thought made me a little sick.

"Dang it," I said. I hated these feelings rolling around inside me. I hated being confused and feeling lost and alone. And still, somehow, feeling free. I felt crazy.

"What?" Cara asked. We were at the top of the driveway now.

I pulled my bike to a stop at the entrance and looked down the shady lane. The trees grew thick all alongside the property. A barbed-wire fence marked our boundaries. I couldn't see over the hill down to the house. Was Mom there? I felt my stomach lurch at the thought. Was the lurch from happiness or from being afraid?

"Why'd you say 'dang it'?" Cara asked.

"Because I don't know what to do."

"About what?"

"About living, Cara. How long do you think this money will last?"

"I know you're worried about that, Caity. But there are places to go if we need help."

"Sure there are. There are children's homes." My voice was sarcastic.

"There are other places. I read this book *Homecoming*. The girl in there walks a long, long way with her brothers and sister. They're going to their grandmother."

"I talked to you about Nana already. You said you didn't want to go there. Have you changed your mind? Or are you thinking about your dad's mother? She lives in Idaho. Either place is a long walk." I was feeling frustrated. Being hungry and afraid to go home didn't help any.

"No. I'm saying that they made it on less money than we have. They went a long way."

"But Cara, they were going somewhere. They were ending up someplace. They were going to someone who would help them. We're not. We're staying here. And besides, that book was just a story."

"Maybe." Cara smiled at me.

"If we go anywhere," I said, ignoring her smile, "it'll be to Nana's. Especially if we're walking."

"It'd be easier to think of jobs," Cara said.

"You're making me crazy," I said. And it really felt that way. All crazy and mixed up.

"Maybe we could get a housecleaning job. We could let them see inside the fridge. They'd hire us just like that." Cara snapped her fingers.

I laughed then. It was a laugh that broke up a little worry and sent it flying into the Parson Brown orange tree grove that was part of our land. Getting up all my strength, I pushed off down the driveway, riding the hand brake the whole way, waiting to see the rusty blue Escort come into view. Afraid that I would. Afraid that I wouldn't.

But there was nothing there under the trees, except two squirrels out playing late.

I heaved a sad sigh of relief that I didn't know all the answers about my mother. Then Cara and I went inside so we could make dinner.

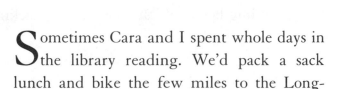

CHAPTER
THIRTEEN

Sometimes Cara and I spent whole days in the library reading. We'd pack a sack lunch and bike the few miles to the Longwood City Library.

"I want a good book," I'd say to Janet, one of my favorite librarians.

"Have you read all the Newberys?" she'd ask.

"A couple, in school last year." Mr. Cannon's English class seemed very far away to me now. Almost like it was a memory in a gray fog.

"There's the whole shelf of them. Start from the most recent and read backward."

"Good idea," I said, even though I wasn't sure why. But I did what she said, checking out an armload of books. For days after, I'd float in the boat with Cara, reading about different times or different places or different people. Or we'd sit out under the oaks and read, books spread out around us.

"Have you read Betsy Byars? She's funny. How about Bill and Vera Cleaver? They write about Florida, did you know that? There's Alane Ferguson. She writes mysteries. And don't forget Roald Dahl. If you haven't read *Fantastic Mr. Fox*, you should," Janet would say, pulling books off the shelves and stacking them in my waiting arms.

Our backpacks weighed more when we came back from the library than they did when we came back from food shopping.

Sometimes Cara and I spent whole days with Brandon.

"Let's go to my house for lunch, Caity," he'd say every once in a while. "My mom's home. You know how she likes to talk to you. Cara can come, too."

"Does she know anything?" I'd ask. "About Mom, I mean."

"No," Brandon would say, shaking his head. And his hair, which was growing longer because it was summer, would shine in the sunlight, brown like a deer.

Lunch was always good, always homemade, always a lot. Mrs. Hill would smile at us and ask me questions about Mom while Brandon was showing off in the pool.

Sometimes Cara and I spent the whole day dreaming of life being different. Mom was home and nice. Or the phone worked and we called Nana to let her know we missed her. Or our fathers each sent us a huge box, as big as the fridge, full of presents.

But always, in the back of my mind, was the thought of how much money we had left. Some nights I'd even dream that I'd lose the last few dollars, that the pennies would fall down the drain in the kitchen and I wouldn't be able to get them out.

Saturdays were the best shopping days because there were so many people at Piggly Wiggly. We could go back more than once to the different taste tables. It was on a Saturday that we spent our last eight dollars.

"What should we get?" I asked Cara. I was scared, scared because somehow this seemed like the end. We couldn't live without food. Mom wasn't coming back anytime soon. Suddenly I was angry. In the seafood section, next to the krab salad taste test place, I became very angry. Standing there in front of the big glass box that held the lobsters with their claws tied, I became very, very angry.

I wanted to run screaming through the aisles. I wanted to grab boxes and bags and cans of food and throw them into a cart. I wanted a candy bar.

Why were we alone? Why had Mom left? Why did I have to be scared all the time?

I watched the lobsters, their eyes out on stems, and clenched my fists. Then I started crying.

"What is it?" Cara asked. For the first time since Mom had left she sounded worried.

About time, I thought. I shouldn't have to do all the worrying alone.

"Are you hurting somewhere?"

I shook my head, then I nodded. Then I shook my head again. I was too confused to even know how to answer. That made me all the madder.

"What, Caity?" Cara was sounding panicked. "What's wrong?"

I took a deep breath and turned to my sister. Her face was red. She was crying now.

"What's wrong?" Cara reached out and took hold of my hand.

The lady behind the lobsters looked at us, worried. "Are you girls okay?" she asked. "Is someone following you? Has someone hurt you?" She walked quickly around to us.

It's my mom, I wanted to say. It's my mom who's hurt us. But I didn't.

"Are you lost?" the Lobster Lady asked. She smelled like fish. Her arms were fleshy and her eyes were puffy and she seemed to really care.

"I can't find the milk," I sobbed.

"Oh, honey," she said, wrapping her arms around me. Her voice was as soft as her skin. "It's on the opposite side of the store."

"Thank you," I said, sniffling. I pulled away and took Cara's hand. I stopped crying. With a big breath, I pushed all my sadness and fear deep inside.

We walked to the milk section and got a quart of the no-name-brand stuff. Then we got a dozen eggs and found the basket with the discontinued and dented stuff in it. There were two cans of kidney beans for only twenty-eight cents each. It's amazing how good kidney beans taste when you're really hungry. A small package of rice, celery, day-old bread, two bananas and four cucumbers at four for a dollar left us with just enough money for a small jar of peanut butter. We had ninety-three cents left.

We were packing up the backpacks when Cara said, "Caity, I saw candy bars for twenty-five cents each."

I glanced at my sister. She was busy putting things from her bag into her pack. She looked too thin to me. A breeze blew past us, smelling of the day and the parking lot. A small zephyr caught up candy wrappers and danced them away from us.

"What kind?" I asked.

"The Nestlé kind."

"Stay here," I said.

I left Cara to finish packing the food. And I went

back into the cool of the store. Someone announced a sale on salmon and I wondered if it was the Lobster Lady. The voice sounded a little bit like her.

In the candy aisle I picked out three candy bars, two Baby Ruths and a Butterfinger. I couldn't wait to get out of the store.

Cara stood waiting. I handed her the candy.

"You wasted," she said, and tore open the wrapper.

"I wasted," I said. "I wasted our last dollar." I opened my candy, too, saving the Butterfinger for later. With the first bite I felt like I was in Willy Wonka's chocolate factory. I knew exactly how Charlie felt when he bit into *his* first bite of chocolate. I couldn't remember anything ever tasting so good.

I looked at Cara.

"I'm glad you wasted," she said, and I grinned at her.

CHAPTER

FOURTEEN

A couple of days later a car pulled into our driveway.

I was sitting in the living room, reading, when I heard two doors shut. My heart started pounding. Cara came running from the bedroom.

"Someone's here," she said. Her face looked white.

"Is it Mom?"

"I didn't look."

"I heard two doors close." We were whispering, crouched down in the middle of the room.

Someone knocked. I looked at Cara wide-eyed.

"Caity." It was Brandon.

I stood up, relieved, my arms and legs shaking.
The knock came again.

I ran to the door and opened it. There stood Brandon and his mom. They held two large paper bags.

"We're going away for a while. We thought you guys could use this stuff that was in our fridge," Brandon said, and he started walking up the steps without waiting for me to ask him in. Thank goodness the kitchen was straightened.

I smiled at him as he walked past.

"Do you think your mom will mind?" Mrs. Hill asked.

"No ma'am. I don't think she will mind at all," Cara said.

Mrs. Hill waited on the bottom step. "I didn't want these things to spoil, and then Brandon suggested we give them to your family." She pushed the groceries toward me and I took the bag from her. It was heavy.

"He sure is a thoughtful young man, isn't he?" she asked.

"Yes ma'am," Cara and I said at the same time.

"Caity," called Brandon from the kitchen. I carried the bag in and set it on the counter.

"I wanted to tell you goodbye." He looked at me, his brown eyes big and round. "We're only going to be gone three weeks. But it seems so long now that I like you."

I felt a lump of sadness well up into my throat. I

tried to smile, but my lips quivered. Like when he asked me to the dance, I thought. Only this time I wasn't embarrassed about shaking lips.

Brandon reached his hand out to me. "Come here. I want to tell you bye. Privately." He grabbed my hand and pulled me into the bathroom. I was really glad the shower curtain was closed. He shut the door behind him.

"My mom is worried about me kissing you," he said. His voice was a whisper, close to my ear. His breath was warm. It gave me goose bumps up and down one arm. "I don't want her to peek in on us. She might have a heart attack."

He kissed me then. His lips were soft. I kept my eyes open, wanting to see him every minute until he dissolved into the brown color of his hair.

"Listen," he said. "I'm worried about you and Cara." He hugged me close.

"Don't worry," I said.

"I watch you at night when you go swimming," he said. "From my back porch. I won't be here to do that. Something could happen. There'd be no one for you to call."

"Brandon," I said. "We'll be okay. I promise." I put my nose into his neck.

"Brandon, we've got to go," called Mrs. Hill.

"I'm coming," he said, and squeezed me tight a second time.

"I think I'm going to cry," I said.

"I'll be back."

I nodded. "I know."

"Brandon," Mrs. Hill called.

"It's your mom," I said.

Brandon held on to my hand, and we walked from the bathroom and into the kitchen and out of the house together.

"We'll miss the plane if we don't hurry," Mrs. Hill said. Her eyes were narrowed. My face turned pink. "That food needs to go into the fridge."

"Yes ma'am," I said.

Cara stood quiet beside me. Brandon and his mother walked away. He turned once and waved. We waved back.

We watched them drive away.

"Let's go see what's in the bags," Cara said.

"Thank you," I said to the back of Brandon's car. We were going to live awhile longer.

That night we celebrated our food by skinny-dipping.

The moon hung in the air, large and yellow. The weeds near the banks of the lake were dark. They moved slightly from a breeze that barely touched us, making a rustling sound.

"Look," I said, my towel tightly wrapped around me and tucked under my arms. "The Hills must have their lights on a timer." Floodlights spread out on the back lawn, making everything either very bright or very shadowed.

"This is the first time in a long time that we've been able to skinny-dip," Cara said. "Brandon is over here all the time now."

I grinned, then dropped my towel on a lounge chair and stepped into the water. The hot night air brushed against me, feeling as delicious as I knew swimming would. I slid off into the water and, taking strides with my arms, pulled myself out deep, then turned and came back.

Cara was splashing water onto the slide.

"My butt sticks if the slide's not wet," she said, and I laughed. My voice went off across the lake to find somebody who might be listening.

Night swimming on the lake is like watching a black-and-white movie. Now Cara climbed to the top of the slide, the water shining on her skin. She looked zebralike, dark where she had tanned and light where her bathing suit had covered her. She went down the slide with a "Whoop!," water splashing up around.

I floated on my back and looked at the stars that sprinkled the sky. The smell of honeysuckle came toward me.

Everything was going to be okay, I could see that now. Food had been given to us. Maybe we would stay here on the lake, alone, with Mom gone, and someone would always be there when we needed help. I liked the thought, the way it felt inside my head. I rolled over on my stomach, dove under, then stood in the chest-high water, pushing my hair back off my face.

Everything was quiet. The slide reflected the moon. And for a moment, fear seemed to push in my head, with a strange pressure that made it hard to breathe. My good feeling left.

"Cara?" I started forward, parting the water with my hands. "Cara?" My voice was loud. She would come up any second, I knew. There was no need to worry. "Where are you, Cara?" Now my voice was more than loud. It echoed back and forth across the water. It echoed back and forth in my mind. It made me stop breathing, made me gasp for air.

"Cara!" I screamed, and waited for her to answer from the house where she might have gone to get us lemonade.

There isn't any lemonade, I thought.

"Oh dear God," I said. My sister. Where is my sister? Where should I look for my sister? The slide stood gleaming and I pushed my way to it. I tried to run. My heart felt like it was pounding everywhere in my body. I could feel it in my temples. Behind my eyes. In my wrists. And so hard in my throat and chest that to breathe was nearly impossible.

Maybe she's in the spring, I thought. I could find

her there. It wasn't so deep. I dove into the water at the foot of the slide. It went from warm to cool quickly.

I waved my arms in front of me as I went down deep into the water. Then I came up, my head pounding because I had waited so long for air. I dog-paddled, breathing hard.

"This isn't working. This isn't working!" I screamed.

There was no way I could find her in the spring.

But I had to find her. Now. It would be too late in the morning. It would be too late when I could see. I had to find her now.

Maybe she wasn't here. The lake is too big. I swam away from the slide.

"Dear God. Dear God. Please help me, dear God. Please help me."

I pushed through the water, which seemed to cling to me. I pushed near the slide and there she was. Facedown. Floating just under the waist-deep water.

I grabbed Cara's hair. It felt like wet silk. I pulled her up. Put my arms around her. She was slippery and heavy. How long had she been under? Thirty seconds? Ten minutes?

I pulled her up onto the shore. She seemed so dark on the white sand. Now what should I do? I tried to remember the mannequins from CPR class, but I couldn't remember any but the tiny doll, the baby that

I had grabbed and run around in circles with like I was panicking.

Panicking. Do not panic. That was a class rule.

I felt for Cara's pulse. She had one, though I was surprised that I found anything, the way my fingers were shaking.

But she wasn't breathing.

"Cara, breathe," I said.

Then I bent over to breathe for my sister. Her wet hair was across her mouth, partly covering her face. I moved it away.

Breath, breath, I thought. Then, pause two three four breath breath pause two three four.

"Cara," I said to her still body. "Don't leave me. Don't leave me."

Continue CPR until someone comes to take your place or you cannot do it anymore, my teacher said in my mind. Mr. Alexander, tall and thin, bent over the boy mannequin, telling us to never give up.

No one would ever come to take my place.

I breathed again for Cara. "Don't leave me," I said to her. "I don't want to be here all alone." Breath, breath. I shook Cara. "Nothing is happening. Nothing is happening!" I cried out. Mosquitoes buzzed near my head.

"Help me!" I screamed. I rocked back on my knees and called out to the heavens, cried out to my nana's God. The night seemed very big. And Cara and I were very small. In the night, far away from help. Far away from God. Far away from the moon.

Cara coughed then and tried to roll over. Relief rushed through my body, making my skin feel tingly.

"Thank you, thank you," I said to the night and to God and to the moon. Then I pulled my sister onto my lap and held her, my head close to hers.

"Don't look," she said. "I'm naked."

CHAPTER

FIFTEEN

I cried all the way to the house, and then after we dressed in our nightshirts, I cried some more.

"I don't like this now, Cara," I said, when we snuggled close together in Mom's bed. The clock on the dresser said 2:13. The blue green of the numbers reflected in the mirror. The light from the hall lit up the bedroom a bit.

"You don't like what?"

"Our being alone."

Cara was quiet a minute. "I didn't mean to . . . I slipped when I was standing on the slide and fell. I guess I hit my head. I—"

"Cara, it's been more than a month now. We need to be with someone. Someone who can take care of us. The money Mom left is gone."

"We'll manage."

"How?"

"We got those two bags of food. And there's even meat in there." Cara coughed, then touched her throat with her hand. "It hurts," she said.

"I guess so. You almost drowned. What would have happened if I hadn't taken that CPR class at school?" I moved closer to my sister. Her hair was damp and smelled of the lake. "Listen. We need help. Mom may never come back. What do we do for money? People are not going to keep dropping off bags of food here. That was Brandon's idea. He knew we needed it."

Cara thought for a moment. "What about the two child support checks?"

"They're made out to Mom."

"Well, Caity, lots of kids take care of themselves."

"I know that. But I don't want to be one of those kids."

"And I don't want to be with Mom again. I'm afraid whoever we find will make us go back to her."

I glanced up at the ceiling. The dim light from the hall made a shadow like a monster with his mouth gaping.

"I like it without her," Cara said.

"I do, too, in a way," I said.

"What way?"

"I can't explain it." And I couldn't, either, because I was confused by my own feelings. It was like there was a great big ache sitting all over my body.

"She was always so mean," Cara said. "You and me, we don't fight. We don't yell. No one is telling us that we're ugly and dumb. No one is telling us that they wish we'd never been born. I like the way it feels here at home now. I don't want her to be my mother anymore."

I was quiet. "There are other people," I said at last. I was thinking of the Lobster Lady at the Piggly Wiggly.

"Who? One of our fathers? Mine is always in a different state when we hear from him and yours has another wife and four children. There's no room for us there."

"What about Mom's sister? Or her brother?" I asked. Before Mom stopped seeing everyone, we'd always met with our aunt and uncle. And Nana. At least four times a year. I could still see Aunt Margaret's smiling face. She was so pretty and little. And she had a boy and a girl, just our ages.

"I'm kind of scared of them, because of that fight," Cara said.

"Oh." I knew what she was talking about. The last fight the family had, when Mom ran from the reunion, screaming and crying, dragging us along with her. It seemed like a million years ago.

"Remember how mad everyone was?" Cara asked. "Remember how when we came in the room, everyone was hollering?"

"How could I forget?" That was the truth. How could I forget? Mom's face red as a beet, Nana hushing her, Uncle Ryan pacing, his wife hurrying to clean things up. And Aunt Margaret. She was sitting on the sofa, angry, her jaw working, like she was grinding her teeth to nubs. "Go out, Caity," she had said to me when I came in to ask if the kids could have more pie. "And don't come back in unless we call for you."

Mom went crazy then. She cursed and yelled so loud it hurt my ears, about how she was the only person allowed to boss us around. "Get in the car," she screamed at me. "Find your sister and get in the car."

And that was the last time I had seen any of them, though I did get to talk to Nana every once in a while. I even made arrangements to have Nana sew Mom's school clothes this summer. But that was before everything changed.

"Nana probably wouldn't mind if we came over for a while," Cara said.

I smiled, thinking about Nana. "She doesn't like to drive."

Outside a night storm came toward us. Warm air pushed through the house. The only curtains in the house, the ones in Mom's room, moved with great breaths of air. The storm hit us like it was angry. Rain pounded from the sky. Lightning struck closer and closer.

"I hate storms," Cara cried out. She pulled the covers over her head and curled up like a roly-poly.

I sat like a statue, too afraid to move. Then the electricity went off. First there was the long rectangle of light falling from the hall onto the bedroom floor; then there was nothing but blackness. The blue green of the clock went out, too. A clap of thunder, directly over our heads, rocked us.

"Let me under, too," I shouted at Cara, and tried to pull some covers over myself. But Cara was wrapped up like a cocoon.

I butted up against her, on my knees, my arms wrapped over my head. Thunder crashed around us.

And for some reason, I remembered my grandmother when I was very young. Out at her house, which she later sold. Watching with her as a storm came in from the ocean.

"See, Caity, baby," she said in my memory. "Here it comes." The trees in the yard bowed before the storm. Everything looked very green. Even the sky seemed to have changed colors. "We're safe inside," Nana said. Lightning crackled and popped. The trees swayed. The rain came down, large, fat drops that made huge puddles in the yard. And Nana, her arms wrapped around me tight, talked about God and how He was giving everything, big and small, something to drink.

With a bang, Mom had come into the room then, and shouted about Nana teaching me things about God.

"I don't believe. Neither should she," she said. And with a jerk, sent me spinning away from my grandmother.

What a funny memory, I thought, knowing I hadn't really been spinning like a top but remembering it that way.

Around us, now, the storm slowed and only rain fell. Cara loosened in her cocoon and finally fell asleep. She wouldn't give up the covers, though.

And I thought of Nana and Mom and being alone on the lake until finally I slept, too.

CHAPTER

SIXTEEN

We slept late.

When I opened my eyes, the clock and its reflection were flashing 88:88. Birds sang. Everything seemed clean and fresh. And I had an idea.

Quietly I rolled out of bed. There was leftover ham in the fridge now, thanks to Brandon. That would be a good thing to fry up for breakfast. A final breakfast on the lake, if Cara agreed.

In the kitchen, I sliced up ham and mixed eggs to scramble. Then I poured two glasses of milk. We could drink this all before we left. And make sandwiches to take. And there were Pop-Tarts, brown sugar cinnamon ones. We could take two backpacks full of

our clothes and tie our lunches to the bikes somewhere.

The ham sizzled in the pan. It popped and crackled. The smell was so good my mouth watered and
my stomach growled.

"Hey," said Cara. She stood in the kitchen doorway. Her hair looked like a rat's nest, probably because she had slept with it wet.

"Hey," I said. "You hungry?"

She nodded and padded into the room.

"Set the table and we'll eat in a few minutes," I
said.

Cara went about doing what I had told her. She
was quiet and so was I. Only the ham made noise,
spitting in the pan.

I opened the oven. It was dark with food that had
been spilled in it and cooked onto the walls and
bottom. I knew it would smoke if I used the broiler,
but there had been a half loaf of sourdough bread
and two sticks of butter in the bag of food. Toast
sounded good to me. Anyway, we would need a big
breakfast.

In my mind, I floated with last night's memories.
My body seemed to sway the way it did when I lay on
my back in the water and stared up into the night
sky, watching stars. I could almost feel the silk-soft
water against my skin. I closed my eyes to the mem-

ory, but that only made it worse. I put four pieces of bread, with globs of butter on them, into the oven and closed the door partway.

Cara sat at the table and watched me.

I turned to her, and opened my arms wide. I felt very old, like I was carrying a heavy bag on my shoulders.

Cara pushed her chair back. It squeaked against the yellow linoleum. She walked over and put her arms around my waist, resting her head near my own. My nose was at the level of her hair. I closed my eyes and the lake smell of her hair floated me to the water again. I hugged my sister tight and for some reason my heart ached.

We stood in the kitchen, hugging, for only a few moments. Then I smelled the sweet smell of cooking butter.

"Time to eat," I said into Cara's hair.

She went to the table and I brought over her food.

"I've decided something," I said as we ate. The ham was just-right salty. The eggs were soft and tasted good on the toast. The milk was cold. It seemed the perfect last meal.

Cara nodded. "I know."

"I want us to leave."

Cara nodded again.

"Do you know where I want us to go?"

"No."

I took a deep breath. "To Nana's."

Cara nodded.

I was surprised she didn't fight me.

"It's a long way," I said.

"We can take our bikes."

"It takes a couple of hours in the car. We'll leave after breakfast. We should be there by tonight."

We ate the rest of the meal in silence. I watched my sister, loving her so much right then that it made it hard to swallow.

We washed the dishes and went to pack our things.

"Take only what you need," I said. "We have a long way to go."

I packed as fast as I could. My drawing things were most important. A few pairs of underwear and three T-shirts. Socks. Two pairs of shorts. My toothbrush. We were out of toothpaste and had been for what seemed like forever. Maybe Nana would have some.

Mom always said Nana didn't like us. She wouldn't let us stay with her.

"Stop," I said out loud. "Do not think of anything." I started humming a made-up song, but still Mom's words came to my mind. "She likes you even less than I do."

"Brandon, Brandon, Brandon," I chanted. And that helped.

Then I went to pack food, anything and everything I could squeeze into my backpack. The few apples, the last of the sliced ham, some cheese. I took a plastic Piggly Wiggly bag and put a few more things in it: the Pop-Tarts, some oranges, three bananas, sweet-smelling and speckled with brown.

"I'll boil the rest of the eggs," I said when Cara came into the kitchen with her backpack. "And we can take these little bits of sliced meat and make sandwiches along the way." I put the five eggs in water as I spoke, turning the burner on high. We wouldn't be hungry. Maybe it would even last a little while at Nana's.

"What about something to drink?" Cara asked.

"There's that bottle of Sprite."

"How can we carry it?"

I shrugged. "Maybe tie it to one of the bars?"

At last it was time to leave. We had finished the packing. The eggs were still hot in their own little bag. Everything was tied to the bars of the bikes, including the plastic bottle of Sprite.

"Wish I had one of those granny baskets," Cara said. "That would make it easier."

We stood out near the garage. The smell of mold came from inside it. A slight breeze rustled the leaves. Already it was hot out. I had pulled my hair back into a long ponytail and then done the same for Cara.

"I think we should tell things goodbye," I said.

I walked to the block wall and stood up on it. I looked toward Brandon's house. I looked where we played baseball. I could see the old pillowcase somebody had stolen from their house to make a second base.

The sky was very blue, the sun almost straight overhead. I looked out at the lake, where parts of it reflected the sky. Little chips of diamonds seemed to float on a wavy section of water. Farther from me the lake was still and looked like a mirror. And then I saw the slide, silver and cold-looking near the shore. My stomach felt sick.

I turned and made my way up to Cara.

"Let's go," I said.

CHAPTER

SEVENTEEN

▼

I had been to Nana's house enough to know that we wouldn't get lost. But it would take us awhile. At least until that evening. There was a long strip of road that edged fields of cabbage and pastures where cows grazed that we'd have to travel over. That would be after getting through Longwood and Sanford.

I thought of this as we stood at the top of our driveway.

I glanced sideways at my sister. "Can you do it?"

"Of course."

"Even after last night?"

"Yes."

"Okay. You follow me, then, until we're on

the old highway. Then I think we can ride side by side."

I pushed off down the road. I could hear the whir of Cara's bike behind me.

Longwood was busy. I wasn't sure what day it was, but I hoped it wasn't Saturday. If it was, then the whole way to New Smyrna would be crowded with people headed to the beach. Traffic on that narrow two-lane road could get dangerous. I remembered hating the drive with Mom. People passing each other. I was always afraid someone would crash head-first into us. And on the days Mom was angry, she'd scream at Cara and me. Hitting at us as she drove, weaving in and out.

At Longwood Hills Road, Cara and I turned left. There were a few cars, but not that many. The sun reflected off the blacktop, shining heat into our faces. The air was hot as well. It wasn't but a half hour we'd been traveling and I was already sweating up a storm.

We followed Longwood Hills Road out to 17-92. I stopped at the light that would let us out onto the highway. Now there were lots of cars. And they were going fast. Cara pulled up alongside me.

"This is going to take us forever," she said.

"Be glad we don't have to climb any real hills."

"I am."

The light changed from red to green, and I pedaled

out with the traffic. Someone behind me beeped, and I pulled off into the grass at the side.

"We're never gonna get there if you keep stopping," Cara said.

"I know that." I was suddenly irritated with her. I was hot, my legs were tired, sweat ran down my back and under my arms and off my head and into my eyes. "I stopped to tell you something."

"What?"

"Stay on this side of the yellow line." I pointed to the side closest to the grass. "I hate being beeped at, and I think we'll be safer."

"Well, in school, a policeman came to my classroom and talked about bicycle safety. He said we have the same rights as cars."

A semi roared past us. The air swirled up and around, hot and smelly.

"That might be, but they're bigger and go faster, so I think we need to be as careful as possible. Stay as far to the right as you can."

"Okay, Caity."

Cara's voice let me know she was going to try. It made all my bad feelings disappear.

"Okay," I said. I waited for a break in the traffic, and we started down the long busy highway toward Sanford. That was where I planned for us to take our first break.

I was wrong about there being no hills in Florida. Highway 17-92 was a gradual slope that I thought would never end. My leg muscles burned from the strain of pedaling. My head hurt from the effort of concentrating on the yellow line so I wouldn't get squished. My nose and eyes burned from the fumes of cars and trucks that passed us. Everything hurt from the whole awful ride.

When we got into Sanford, we stopped at the first 7-Eleven on 17-92.

"Don't ask for anything," I said as we parked our bikes. "We don't have even one red cent. You go in first and cool off. Use the bathroom and take your time. I'll watch our bikes."

While Cara went into the store, I untied the bottle of Sprite. It exploded when I loosened the lid, spraying me, my bike and the sidewalk with foam.

"Yuck," I said. If being hot and sweaty wasn't bad enough, I would now be sticky. I drank down the soda as fast as I could until my stomach ached. It burned the back of my throat, but I was no longer thirsty.

And we wouldn't be hungry, either, I thought, looking at the bags tied to our bike bars.

I eased my backpack to the ground. We'd eat what was in there first, I decided. I didn't want to carry any more weight than I had to. My back itched where the pack had rested. I wondered if my shirt was all wet, how far we had come, and how long before we would get to Nana's place.

Cara came outside and I handed her the drink. "I'll be right back," I said.

And I went into the store. The air was cool on my face and cooler still on my sweaty body. Already the soda was drying on my hands, making them feel sticky.

I went into the bathroom and washed up my face and hands. I splashed water under my arms and down my neck. I washed the syrup from my legs, where it had dried in shiny, small circles. Then I dried off with a bunch of paper towels and went back outside to Cara.

"We'll eat outside of Sanford," I said.

Cara nodded. Her face was red from working so hard.

We started off again.

Now the traffic was heavier. In the 7-Eleven I had noticed it was after two. Cars poured out of the road that led to the community college. That meant it wasn't Saturday. Good.

"When I sell my first book," I remembered Mom saying once when she hadn't been angry, "I'll go to work for the college. All colleges like to have published teachers." Thinking of her dreams made me feel sad.

It seemed to take forever to get into the heart of Sanford. Then we were stopping and starting, pushing off and pedaling like crazy to get through the city. Past the fast-food restaurants, which sent out smells of chicken and hamburger and grease. Through the lights, past the grocery stores and churches, to the light that would lead us out of Sanford and to Nana's house.

The sun was starting to ease down toward the west when we stopped to eat at an abandoned gasoline station.

I was too tired to talk. I could hardly uncurl my fingers from around the handlebars, I was so tired. I handed Cara the fruit from my backpack. We ate the sandwiches and the boiled eggs, though I wondered how I'd even pick off the shell. We drank the last of the soda. After we were through eating, we gathered the trash and dumped it into an empty blue can that was grimy with oil.

"Let's just sit," Cara said. "For only a few minutes."

I didn't have the energy to argue. I plopped down on the concrete where pumps had once been. At least we were in the shade.

Traffic was less busy out on the edge of town where we were now. I watched for Mom's car. Twice I saw ones that looked like hers, but neither was. My arms and legs thumped in a funny way because we had come so far.

"We've got to go," I said at last. "I'll go across the street to that house and see if they'll let me fill this bottle with water from their hose. You stay here."

Cara nodded.

No one was at home, so I went ahead and used the hose to fill the Sprite bottle. Then I drank as much water as I wanted, hoping it would keep me cool and not make me sick. Last of all, I wet my hair and face. We still had a huge amount of pedaling to go.

The edge of Sanford is where the fields begin. The smell of cabbage and dirt was thick in the air. We passed a dead skunk and one squished cat. We passed a sign that said Osteen 16 Miles. Sixteen more miles. I knew this was the beginning before a very long end, but I didn't know if I could make it.

Cara looked as tired as I felt.

"We're almost there," I said to her over my shoulder. "We only have a few more miles."

Cara didn't say anything.

It took us forever to get to the tiny town of Osteen. Mostly what we saw there was dogs. And lots of dead animals, some mashed so badly I couldn't even tell what they had started out as.

We stopped to rest. Up ahead I could make out the road that would eventually get us to New Smyrna. If we didn't wind up like the armadillos and skunks we were passing. Squished flat. There was a big green sign there.

We drank water and sat and sweated.

When she could breathe without gasping, Cara asked, "What if she won't take us?"

"She will," I said.

"She might not."

"She will when we tell her we're alone."

Cara looked off toward the east. We sat in front of a deep irrigation ditch. Water trickled through it. Weeds were high there.

Cara shrugged.

"Imagine getting into one of Nana's beds," I said. "Think how good we're going to sleep."

CHAPTER

EIGHTEEN

The sign at the turn said forty-five miles before we got to New Smyrna.

"Forty-five damn more miles," I said. " 'Scuse my French."

"I'm telling Mom you cursed," Cara said. Then she grinned.

"If you could only find her," I said. "Let's get going. The first person who sees the flashing stoplight at the end of this road wins a prize."

"What?"

"A candy bar maybe."

We both knew there wasn't any money for candy bars but set off pedaling fast and furious.

We hadn't gone far when a red convertible went past us, beeping.

I swerved closer to the edge of thc road. Somebody threw a bottle out the window. It bounced along the grass and landed near a wooden fence post.

"Jerk," I said under my breath. I wanted to yell it out, but that could be stupid. There were miles to go before we would come to any houses. And already the sun was looking for a place to rest for the night. We had a long way to go alone. I didn't need to draw any attention to us.

In the field to the left, I saw a big pig-looking thing.

"Cara," I said, pulling to the side of the road. "Look at the size of the pig."

She stopped, too, and we gazed out across the field. The pig looked back at us. "It's a boar," Cara said.

"Can he get through the fence?" I asked, but Cara was moving up the road.

I pulled my bike alongside hers, breathing hard.

Cara slowed her pumping. I kept pace beside her, dropping behind whenever I heard a car coming up.

Cows grazed in the pastureland next to us. We passed small clumps of trees, then larger groups. Once we went past a lake. It shone sparkly in the distance.

The air was cooler now. Big bugs flew heavy in the air around us. Every once in a while, one would smack me in the face or chest. I hoped none of them could sting.

"We're coming up on that one big farmhouse," I

said. "Remember? Mom used to pretend that she owned it. Remember how we would describe our bedrooms with all the nice furniture?"

A car came toward us. It moved fast.

"Single file," I said. My heart started thumping, though I wasn't sure why. "Don't stop unless I tell you."

"All right, Caitlynne," Cara said, and she fell behind me.

I rode the white line that marked the side of the road. The car drove by. It was the same red one from before. Why was it back? Somebody yelled out. I pedaled faster.

"Hurry, Cara," I said over my shoulder.

"I am," she said.

The car screeched to a halt. Then with a whining sound, the driver started backing up.

"Faster," I said to Cara.

"I am."

We stayed ahead of the car only a short distance. Soon it was driving backward alongside us.

A guy leaned out the window. "Going my way?" he asked.

I ignored him.

"Going my way?" he asked again. Somebody in the backseat laughed.

The farmhouse was growing closer.

"Here comes a car," someone in the convertible said. The driver slammed on the brakes and, with a burst of speed, squealed up the road.

"Go as fast as you can," I said to Cara. "They'll be back."

I stood to pedal, making sure Cara stayed close behind me. After a few minutes the car *was* back. This time going the same way we went.

"Hey, you two wanting to get somewhere?" The guy in the passenger seat seemed to fill the window. His face was covered with zits and he wasn't wearing a shirt. "We'll take you wherever you want to go."

"No, thank you," I said. "We live right up there." I nodded toward the farmhouse.

A kid in the back laughed. "No, you don't."

I didn't answer.

"What would you say if I told you *I* lived there?" It was the driver of the car. He steered with one hand and leaned toward Cara and me, across the passenger seat.

"I'd call you a liar," I said. I looked the zit-faced guy right in the eyes and didn't flinch.

"Come on, Jennifer," I said back to Cara. "Mom's probably worried." I swung behind the car and over to the opposite lane. Cara followed me.

Just a little bit farther, I said in my mind. Please, please let there be someone home.

"Come on," the driver said. "We'll have us a good old time. We got us something to drink. You're both looking hot and tired."

"You know you don't live there," someone in the back said.

I jerked the handlebars and turned onto the blacktop that led down to the house Mom always wanted to own.

The car followed us halfway. Then it turned around and parked at the end out by the road.

Cara and I pulled into the garage, where we got off our bikes. My legs were shaking and so were my hands. A blue Jeep was parked catty-cornered there. A big white freezer was against one wall with two signs over it. One said It's Miller Time. The other said Fitsgibbons Live Here.

"Come on," I said.

Steps led to the back door. A button that looked like a doorbell was near the freezer. I pressed it. The garage door began to close. It made a lot of noise.

"Oh no," I said. For a moment I couldn't move.

"Knock," Cara said.

I did, all the while watching as the metal door made its way down.

There were footsteps coming from inside the house. The door swung open and there stood a wide-eyed old woman.

"What are you doing in my garage?"

"Hiding," I said. "Some guys were chasing us. . . ."

Cara burst into tears.

The woman eyed Cara for a long moment. Then she pressed the garage door open. It squeaked and groaned all the way up.

The red car waited. I pointed with my finger. "They're following us," I said.

The woman stepped out of her house to see better. Cara continued to cry, but only soft-sounding sniffles.

The woman walked to the mouth of the garage and stood there with her hands on her wide hips.

Somebody from the car screamed an ugly name and the car tore away from the driveway, fishtailing as it went.

"Hoodlums," the woman said. She wiped her hands on her blue jeans. It seemed funny to see someone so old wearing Levi's on her bottom half and a T-shirt with faded words on the top half. She turned, then, eyeing us a moment more, said, "Come on in."

CHAPTER
NINETEEN

We called Nana from Mrs. Fitsgibbon's place. Mrs. Fitsgibbon was nice but asked prying questions that I answered only a little.

"Does your mother know you're here?"

"No. We didn't tell her."

"Won't she be angry?"

"Yeah, probably."

"It was a dangerous thing to do."

"I know."

"And your sister couldn't be more than ten."

"She's almost twelve."

"Are you hungry?"

"No ma'am."

"Thirsty?"

"Yes ma'am."

I sat in the front room of Mrs. Fitsgibbon's house. It was big and airy and full of little things.

"My dust collectors," she called them.

She gave us lemonade, then turned on the television. Cara sat on a big brown recliner that had doilies covering the arms and sipped lemonade from a bumpy green glass. I stared out the bay window, watching.

The red car drove past a few times, then after a while it didn't come back at all.

I thought about my grandmother.

In normal life, Mom, Cara and I had visited Nana every two months or so. We'd drive to New Smyrna and spend a few hours until Mom got tired of being there, then we'd drive back to Longwood with Mom vowing we would never visit her mother again. I never knew what went on to make her so angry.

With me, Nana always wanted to know what was going on in school. She'd listened to my times tables, when I was learning them. She showed me a shortcut for doing the nines.

"Why memorize them if they're always at your fingertips?" she had said. And I felt happy, even now, when I used her method. Nana helped me sew my one and only homemade dress that I later accidentally hot-glued at the hem and had to throw away. She let me dog-paddle in her bathtub as long as I cleaned up the splashes, and she didn't even get angry when I picked every periwinkle blossom from the slender plants in her tiny flower garden. Of course I had been young then. It was when I was older that I overheard Nana saying to Mom, "Virginia, if either of those girls come over here to visit covered in bruises again, I will turn you in."

I knew Nana had been talking about calling the police, and I was afraid. That day, when it was time to leave, Nana hugged me close to her, longer than usual. I put my nose into her neck, that smelled like Oil of Olay and cigarettes, and breathed deep.

On the way home that day Cara and I were quiet. Mom cried. The tears trickled slow down her cheeks and dropped off her chin and onto her huge bosom.

"Why are you crying, Mom?" Cara asked.

"I just thought of the most beautiful scene to put into my book." Mom sped the Escort down the highway. "I can't wait to write it."

When we got home that evening she said, "You know I'm a good mother. You two believe that, don't you?"

I nodded, wide-eyed. Cara looked at the ground.

"I never beat you with a belt, do I?"

"No, Mom. You don't," I said.

"That makes me a better parent. As long as I never beat you with a belt, I'm a good mom. Don't you think so?"

"Yes," I said. And I meant it. I felt really glad that Mom didn't own any belts, too. Just in case.

All that time Cara kept quiet.

Now, a car turned down the long driveway and headed to the farmhouse, the headlights cutting a path ahead of it. I stood. Mrs. Fitsgibbon looked at me.

"She's here, I think," I said. My heart started thumping.

Nana had no idea why we were at this house, or why she was picking us up.

I was nervous to see her after such a long time. Nervous to see her in case Mom was right about our grandmother not wanting us. It was dark. The trees in the distance were dark. The sky was a deep blue. The air was very warm.

I stood in the doorway, watching, to make sure. It could be the red car. The floodlights flicked on, lighting things. It was Nana. I ran out to meet her.

She smiled at me and rolled the window down. It squeaked and I wondered if it would even open all the way.

"Sugar," she said, "how are you?"

"Fine." I kissed her puckered-up lips. "We have our bikes."

Nana's eyebrows arched high.

Mrs. Fitsgibbon came outside then, and so did Cara. We pulled our bikes out of the garage and put them both in the trunk. The wheels stuck out some and Mrs. Fitsgibbon gave us rope to tie things down.

Nana talked with Mrs. Fitsgibbon awhile longer, even after Cara and I were in the car.

"What do you think?" Cara asked.

"About what?"

"About Nana taking us?"

"I'm crossing my fingers," I said. "Even though it hurts to from hanging on that old bike."

"Me too, then," said Cara.

We waited, nervous and hot, in the car.

When she finally made her way to us, Nana laughed, then hugged Mrs. Fitsgibbon.

"Think they set a dinner date?" I asked Cara. The car smelled musty. It reminded me of Nana, of times before, times Cara and I spent out in the driveway, pretending to drive this big old thing. The dashboard was covered with a thick layer of dust, like always.

"Well, you know Nana. Mom always said she loved everybody better than us."

Nana got into the car then. The door closed with a rusty sound. After a couple of tries, the engine started. The car shuddered, then backed up to a huge oak tree where a tire swing hung. Nana put the car into forward and we were off to New Smyrna.

CHAPTER

TWENTY

It didn't take us any time at all to get to Nana's house in the car. Especially since the whole ride over, all Cara and I did was answer questions.

"What were you doing way out in the middle of nowhere?"

"Coming to your place."

"My house? What does your mother think of that?"

"She didn't know."

"Why?"

"She's gone."

"Gone? Where?"

"We don't know. Just gone."

The Duster moved along the road. It was night. There were no streetlights, so things seemed especially dark.

Nana lit up a cigarette with a match. The flame wavered a bit from the wind that came in my window. Her face looked orange as she steered with her knee.

"When did she leave?"

"The day school got out."

"My lord, that's more than two months ago. What was she thinking about?"

Nana didn't want us to answer this part of the question. I sat in the car, cigarette smoke filling my nose, and felt comfortable in her horror, maybe like a kitten feels when its mother washes it. I liked it that she worried. It felt strange and warm.

"Who took care of the two of you?"

"We did."

"Who cooked?"

"We did."

"What did you do for money?"

"Mom left some."

"How much?"

"About forty dollars."

"Forty dollars?" Again Nana sounded surprised. She clicked her tongue. She shook her head.

"We were hungry some," I said, hoping that Nana would soothe me a bit more with her words. She did.

"Why didn't she call me?"

"I don't know."

Cara elbowed me in the side.

I closed my mouth tight.

"So why did you wait so long to call? And why did you try and bike over? You should have called."

"We didn't have a phone," Cara said.

"And Cara almost drowned," I said.

"What?" Nana's voice was loud, but nothing like Mom's had ever been. It was a worried sort of holler.

We explained what had happened, leaving out the part about being naked.

Nana stopped at the flashing caution light. We were in Samsula. Only sixteen miles to go, I thought. Only now the miles didn't matter. I leaned my head on the seat and relaxed. Cara could answer questions for a while. I wanted to rest. The wind blew into my face, warm night air. I could smell the faint odor of the ocean, salty and wet. Nana didn't know yet about how Cara and I wanted to live with her.

Up ahead was the 7-Eleven that made me always think of Nana, because it was only a few miles from her house. As we passed, I saw that gas pumps had been put in front. I wondered when. We came to the light at Mission Road. A Wal-Mart sign grew up out of some bushes. This was new too. A lot could happen in only a year, I saw.

Nana turned onto Mission Road. We drove past the place that long ago had been a lake and was now a cow pasture. At the very end of the street was Nana's house. Small and white, hidden partly behind trees that grew thick around the place, huge oaks and a pine or two. The front porch light was on.

Nana drove slowly. She stopped at the corner, even though there was no stop sign, and looked to the left and the right. Only a green sign marked the street. It said E. Lake Drive. I remembered the chant Cara and I sang when we were younger. "Six-oh-five, East Lake Drive, New Smyrna Beach, Flar-ih-duh."

Nana pulled into the driveway and steered into the carport that Uncle Bob and Aunt Carol had given her a few years before for Christmas. Cara was still talking. Nana turned off the Duster. It coughed twice and backfired. A dog down the street started barking.

I looked over at the front porch, painted an olive color to match the eaves of the house. In that Adirondack chair, the one closest to the front door, Mom had sat drinking a large glass of iced tea. It was the Christmas before last. Even though it was more than a year before, I could remember Mom clearly, sipping her tea, calling for Cara and me to hurry up and finish putting the presents in the car so we could go home. It had been a sunny day.

Cara took in a breath and, for a moment, all was quiet, except for the sound of tree frogs.

"We have no place to go," I blurted out. "We wanted to know if we could stay here. I've gotten pretty good at cleaning and I can make pizza from scratch. With or without cheese."

Nana was quiet.

"Without cheese, too?" she asked.

"Yes. It's not as good as the other."

Nana nodded in the dark. The light from the front porch shone into the car a bit, enough for me to see outlines of Cara and my grandmother. An eerie sort of shine seemed to be drawn around their faces. I wondered if I could sketch them, this maybe family.

"My home is your home always."

A horn blared from the road up a ways. If I turned and looked behind me, I knew I would see Wal-Mart. But I didn't. I sat still and heard those words, "My home is your home always," echo in my mind.

CHAPTER

TWENTY-ONE

▼

The house was an old wooden one, with shingles painted white, covering the sides. It sat up on cinder blocks. The porch wasn't screened. Built-in planters nudged up against the house, around the whole front, and here Nana had planted roses. Big roses that smelled strong in the day and even stronger on a hot and heavy night. Roses bursting with color that I tried to echo on my drawing page with pencils I bought from Wal-Mart. Yellow petals that somehow bled into orange and then became pink.

The front yard was small, and a horseshoe-shaped driveway made its way through thick grass. In between two large oaks squatted three round cement planters, fashioned after urns. They were empty, except for dead leaves. Cara and I sat up in two of these and watched the traffic pass at the light, far away down at the corner, before it became evening and mosquitoes went to work for the night. We counted cars. I kept an eye out for Mom.

Nana had her own routine, and Cara and I did our best to settle into it. Every morning we watched television. First, game shows.

"Get me up on that stage," Nana said that first morning we watched with her. She sipped a second cup of coffee while we all lounged in the small family room, near the fireplace. "I could guess the pants right off that ol' gal."

"I hope not," I said.

"Why, I could. I'm the best darn guesser in the state."

And Nana was. She was especially good at coffee prices.

The next morning program was one where the people dressed up crazy. Cara and I learned to hurry and wash dishes during commercials. Nana cleaned at the same time, making beds and putting underwear to soak in the bathroom sink because there was no washer and dryer here. Then she'd pull dinner out of the freezer at the end of the hall and set it to thaw on the kitchen counter.

141

"Let's vote who looks most silly," Cara said.

"The hot dog man."

"No, the garbage bag lady."

"I hope they choose the number eighteen. I'm feeling in my bones that's the one today," Nana said. She kept a list of every grand prize she ever won. "From the comfort of my own rattan chair and without ever having to dress up like a fool."

So far Nana had won vacations all over the world, 163 new cars, 89 new boats, 41 dream houses, 53 vacation homes, 105 new kitchens and tons of washers and dryers.

"We're set for life," she said after every show, licking the pencil lead and writing down the official winnings of the day.

Next we watched the soaps: *The Young and the Restless, General Hospital, The Breaking Hearts, As the World Turns, Days of Our Lives* and *Finders of Lost Love*. This meant switching back and forth between channels but was well worth the effort because then we could watch everything.

"Isn't he a handsome young man? Nearly as nice as he is pretty," Nana said about Alphonsus on *Finders of Lost Love*. I had to agree. Cara liked Crevan better, even though he was the bad guy on *The Breaking Hearts*.

"Crevan is a fiend from Hades who needs to find himself a church to spend a few Sabbath days in,"

Nana said every time we switched to that program and the camera zoomed in close enough to count the pores in his nose. Cara didn't care.

Every Tuesday and Thursday was the same. Visiting Day. We always walked. Nana went in bare feet. She wore a lightweight cotton shirt, and she always wore a pair of polyester pants, no matter how hard Cara and I begged her not to. Her closet was filled with all the colors of the rainbow in polyester. She kept polyester in business.

"Someone might see you," I said one afternoon. It was a Visiting Day. Afterward we were going to the library. "Mr. Burd might drop ashes from that smelly old cigar on you. Polyester melts, you know."

Nana smiled. Today her pants were pale pink. They were snug on her chunky legs.

"Don't they itch, Nana?" Cara asked.

Nana smiled bigger. She kept on walking. The polyester said *swinch, swinch*, with every step. I felt real happy I was wearing cutoffs.

We went to Miss Taylor's house first. Miss Taylor was really old. Her hair, just a few white strands, tried to cover a very pink scalp. She was a tiny thing, and she walked with a walker.

"Maud?" Nana called through her screen door. "You home?"

"She never goes anywhere," I said, "except to Nana's."

"I'm in the kitchen, Doris."

"See?" I said.

"My grandchildren and I are here to visit."

"Oh good, come in, girls." Miss Taylor dipped snuff, so she carried a baby food jar covered with aluminum foil everywhere she went. That was so she'd have a good place to spit. It was pretty disgusting, but at least the glass was covered, so we didn't have to see that stuff sloshing around.

"I'm here to give you your makeover, Maud," Nana said.

Nana went into the bathroom and got bobby pins for the eight strands of baby-fine white hair on Miss Taylor's head. She washed the little lady's scalp till the pink was shiny, then pinned curls all over. Cara and I sat and watched. It was a miracle what Nana could do. When the hair was dry and all the bobby pins removed, Nana puffed up the eight curled strands till they became a tiny white halo.

Then we went to visit Mr. Burd.

Mr. Burd lived on the other side of Nana, two houses down. A sign hung on his door. It said Burd's Roost. Drop-ins Welcome.

"Hello, Frank," Nana shouted at Mr. Burd.

Cara and I could talk in a normal tone of voice, and as long as Mr. Burd didn't see our mouths working, he never knew we were even carrying on a conversation without him. He had fought in every major war since the dawn of time and was nearly deaf. He was also missing three fingers from one hand and a thumb from the other.

"Grenade!" he had shouted at me the first time we'd stopped in. He waved his fingerless hand under my nose like a fan and I nearly screamed.

"Why?" I asked, when what I really meant was, What happened? I was too surprised to form a sense-making question.

"I said, 'grenade,' " he yelled at me that afternoon, even louder than before, as if I was the person who was nearly deaf.

"Oh," was all I could say. But then I wondered: Had he caught the grenade? Not thrown it fast enough? Made the whole story up?

Mr. Burd's remaining stubs were fat and sausage-like. A little bit of black wiry hair grew on stubs and whole fingers alike. I didn't want to look, but time and again I found myself staring at what was left of his hand, hoping it never happened to me. How would I draw if it did?

"My granddaughters and I have come to help you," Nana said in a loud voice. We came here twice a week, too. "They've come to help me clean up your place."

Mr. Burd followed close behind us, shouting instructions as we cleaned his home. He said the same things every time.

"Now don't tuck my covers too tightly around the mattress, Doris. I may have served in the military, but I like my feet free."

"Don't give those geraniums too much water, they'll drown."

"Plump those sofa pillows good. I want to feel comfortable when I'm watching the six o'clock news."

"That old coot," I said when I was washing out the bathtub. If I was going to clean his house, I sure as heck didn't want him yelling at me the whole time.

Nana was squirting Sno Bowl into the toilet.

"Don't forget to rinse out the grit from that Ajax," he shouted at me. His voice slapped against the tile walls. "I hate taking a bath sitting on all that grit. You left too much in last time. It gave me a rash."

I nodded and my hair swung down into my face. I tried not to think of Mr. Burd's butt with a rash on it.

"He's just lonely," Nana said.

"Lonely, baloney," I said. "So what."

"Caitlynne Jackson," Nana said. Her voice was not happy. "He lives all alone. Without a sister to keep him company." She talked without moving her lips so Mr. Burd wouldn't notice she was saying anything.

I looked over my shoulder at the old man. He filled the doorway, his stubby hand resting on the jamb.

My face turned pink at the thought that maybe, by some fluke, he had heard me.

"Thank you," he said, "for doing this." He smiled at me, very un-Mr. Burd-like. His sausage fingers gestured at the bathroom.

I nodded my head and looked into the tub. There was some grit left. I turned on the water and, with my hand, sloshed it around.

I glanced up at Nana. She was staring holes right into me.

"I'm sorry," I said. "I didn't know."

Nana smiled her polyester pants smile, and I knew I was forgiven.

Nana helped everyone in her neighborhood. She didn't always do big things for them, like cleaning their houses or doing hair. Sometimes it was little things like carrying their newspapers to the front porch, or waving, or cooking turnips for somebody.

"Mom was right," I said to Cara. We were sitting in the flowerpots watching traffic move past. "Nana does help everyone. She loves lots of people."

"She's never helped us," Cara said.

"What do you mean?" I asked. "She's letting us stay with her."

"She never did anything before. She never stopped Mom from being so mean."

"Who could stop Mom?" I asked.

"I'm asking her sometime," Cara said. "I'm finding out why Nana never did anything."

I worried about that, but Cara kept her mouth closed tight to those feelings. It was like she was waiting for the right time.

Saturday nights were game nights. Mr. Burd and Miss Taylor walked over to Nana's house because it was the central meeting place. Everybody watched an hour of television, and then we played cards.

Sometimes we played Shanghai, sometimes poker, and every once in a while, we played gin rummy.

Nana and Mr. Burd smoked like chimneys, filling the room with pale-colored smoke that swirled around under the hanging dining room light just like smoke swirls in the movies. The grown-ups drank beer, and Cara and I sipped tea from giant glasses.

One evening I sat out a hand of cards so I could draw a picture. I wanted to sketch the group, especially Mr. Burd holding his cards. I wanted to show the pink and white colors of Miss Taylor's head as she laughed, teeth loose, baby food jar nearby, at something funny Nana had said.

I pulled away from the group and began to draw, wishing for good art supplies.

"What's this hand?" Cara asked. She picked cards from a huge pile spread on the table.

"Two and two," Mr. Burd shouted.

"Two sets, two runs," Nana said. She started stacking the cards into a tall deck that everyone would be able to draw from.

"Two and two," Cara mumbled to herself. And she began to smile as she sorted through her cards.

She must have a joker, I thought.

Smoke hazed the room. Cara's hair grazed the table. Nana laughed a loud laugh, throwing her head back at something Mr. Burd had meant to whisper.

Suddenly I was outside of it all. It was like I was looking at everybody in a photograph. I wasn't a part. I felt like an alien, viewing things in a very different way. The feeling was strange, but I wanted to keep it. I tried not to move so I could keep seeing just as I did now. If I could sketch this scene exactly as I was seeing it . . .

Nana leaned over toward Cara, and my sister laughed, covering her mouth with one hand, holding all her cards in the other.

I was struck to the very heart by Cara. She actually looked happy. I mean, she *was* happy. I couldn't remember ever seeing her this way. She had been content when we had been alone at the lake, content with me. But she never wore a look like the one she had now.

Nana reached toward Cara and pulled her close.

This is good, I thought, our being here. We did need someone after all. We needed to be here, safe. Not with Mom, who beat us up. Just because she was our mother didn't give her the right to pound on us. I saw that clearly at Nana's. And I didn't ache for Mom so much.

I began my drawing.

But I wondered when Cara would talk with Nana and if the conversation would send us off again. Maybe back home to the lake even.

Without really trying, it seemed, Nana worked us right in. The same way that she made Miss Taylor feel good about her balding head and Mr. Burd feel okay even though he was deaf and fingerless.

We're a bunch of misfits, I thought. No fingers, no hair, no mother and polyester pants.

Cara and I talked about Mom with Nana lots. We told her of Mom's anger and her hitting us. We told Nana some of the things that Mom said to us until Nana finally said, "Stop! I can't stand to hear it anymore."

"What, Nana?" Cara asked. "We haven't told you the real mean stuff."

Nana began to cry, without making a sound. Tears slid down her tanned cheeks, following the folds in her skin down to her neck.

I looked hard at Cara. I willed her to look at me. Once I had Cara's eyes on me, I thought, Don't say anything. Don't blame her.

Cara stared down at the table.

"I didn't know how bad it was," Nana said. She

dropped her face into her hands. "I can't bear to hear what she did to you. My poor girls. My poor, poor girls," she said. Then Nana began to cry really hard. "What has happened to my daughter?"

I couldn't tell who she cried the hardest for. Mom or us.

After that, Cara and I talked about Mom alone, when Nana couldn't hear. We worried about the fact that summer was ending.

We talked about swimming, about the big library there in Longwood. And I missed things in my mind: the sun on the lake, the quiet of living so far away from people. The baseball games. And Brandon.

So after I was pretty sure he was home from vacation, I wrote him. He always wrote back and he seemed to be doing good.

CHAPTER

TWENTY-TWO

▼

The last Saturday morning in August, Nana called Cara and me into the hall. She still hung on to the phone, resting it against her hip, until it started beeping. Then she put it back into the cradle.

"That was your aunt Margaret," she said.

My heart started pounding. I wasn't sure why. Aunt Margaret had been over plenty of times even though she lived in Orlando. She and Nana talked on the phone a lot. I couldn't see why I'd be bothered now. Maybe it was Nana's tone.

"Oh?" Cara said. She looked funny around the eyes, like maybe she was afraid of what Nana would say.

"Your mom called her. She's coming home."

"Home where?" I asked. "Here or at the lake?"

"Virginia knows you're here. Margaret told her. But I don't know what your mom plans to do." Nana looked worried. Her eyebrows knit together. She pulled at her short hair, then after a moment, lit up a cigarette.

"What do we do?" I asked. My heart thumped a thick-sounding thump.

"Wait," Nana said.

"I can't go back," Cara said. "I won't go back." She looked over at Nana. "Can I keep staying here? Will you let me?"

Nana moved forward fast, her pants whispering as she walked. Cara stood stiff until Nana put her arms around her and squished her up close.

"I *won't* go back," Cara said. "I won't do it anymore. Mom was mean. I didn't like it there."

"I know," Nana said, crooning into Cara's hair. "It's okay. You both can stay."

We talked long into the day. But Mom didn't come. Aunt Margaret called and said she'd be down if Nana wanted. Nana said no, she thought we'd be okay.

I waited, afraid and excited and confused.

"Maybe things are different," I said to no one, sitting in the flowerpot, watching the cars drive past at the end of the road. "Maybe she's changed. Maybe she needed some time away." The thought of having

153

Mom love me in the right way made my face turn warm.

Mr. Burd came over for dinner, and a little after that, Miss Taylor came by to play cards.

Cara and I hurried and washed the dishes. Nana wiped down the table and put the food away. Miss Taylor clumped around the living room with her walker and baby food jar.

"Rummy, anyone?" Mr. Burd asked.

We all pulled up to the table and began a game.

Aunt Margaret called and said she would be over in a couple of hours after all. Nana told her no, but after a little more conversation, hung up, announcing we would have spend-the-night visitors.

We played cards late into the evening. Miss Taylor left after ten-thirty. Mr. Burd passed a hand for gin rummy. We all listened for Aunt Margaret, knowing she would be here soon.

"Do you think she'll take us back to Mom?" I asked Cara. I had motioned for her to come in the kitchen with me when I went in for more tea for myself and to get Mr. Burd another beer.

"Nah," Cara said, shaking her head.

I looked out the kitchen window. It was dark out-side, and all I could really see was a thin reflection of myself. Just the edges.

Cara opened the refrigerator behind me, and she

became very bright in the window, bending in for a can, coming out again.

We're safe here, I thought.

"She's here," Nana called from the dining room. "Margaret's here."

"Think she brought Jeff and Karen?" I asked, coming in from the kitchen. I sipped a big drink of the icy tea. It was sweet and lemony tasting.

"Maybe," said Nana.

Cara went and looked out through the screen door.

"I hope so." I settled down and picked up my cards.

"It's Mom," Cara said. She turned and ran to me, knocking into the table. "Nanny, it's Mom."

At first I couldn't move. I was frozen.

Nana pushed her chair back and the legs scraped against the wooden floor, squeaking. She walked to the door. "Oh my," she said.

My face felt icy, my skin was numb.

Mr. Burd looked at us all. "We done?" he shouted.

Cara grabbed my arm. She jerked it twice, trying to pull me up, and spilling tea onto my lap.

I stood and Mom appeared at the door.

"Virginia," I heard Nana say. "You're back."

"I've come for my children," Mom said.

"Hide," Cara whispered at me.

Mr. Burd walked to the door, too, and stood a little

behind Nana. He didn't say anything, just waited there, his fingerless hand shoved in a pocket. The hand missing a thumb came to rest on Nana's shoulder.

Cara clutched at my arm and I looked into her face. The old Cara was back, the unhappy Cara.

"Okay," I whispered. Her look made a pain come into my stomach, a pain that even covered up the fear for a moment. "Let's hide."

I scooted out of my chair. I could hear Mom, her voice coming loud from the front porch.

"You've stolen them from me. I could have you put in jail in a second."

"Virginia, you left those children alone for months. . . ."

I tuned Nana out and took Cara's hand. We started walking toward the back door.

"I see them!" Mom's voice was shrill.

Cara bolted from me.

I pulled her back to my side. "Walk quickly," I said. "Don't run. If she thinks we're getting away, she might come around the house."

"I want in," Mom yelled.

I heard the screen door crunch open, but I didn't look to see what was happening behind us. "Now run," I said, and pushed Cara in front of me.

Cara jerked on the doorknob.

"It's locked," I said. "Calm down. We'll make it." My hands fumbled for the top latch.

"Caitlynne! Cara!" Mom's voice was getting close. I could hear her angry stomping through the two rooms that separated us.

"I'm calling the police," Mr. Burd's voice said, and for once it didn't sound like he was yelling.

"Virginia, leave them alone." I could tell Nana was crying. "They want to stay with me."

"You've brainwashed them, then. They've always wanted to be with their mother. I love them and care for them."

The cool lock slid open in my hand. Cara threw the door wide. A rectangle of light spilled down the steps and into the grass. Warm night air, sweet smelling, brushed against my face. My sister stepped outside, her shadow leading the way.

I started to follow, but Mom grabbed me, her hand tight around my arm.

"Go," I screamed at Cara, and she leapt down the rest of the stairs and disappeared into the dark yard.

I twisted this way and that, but Mom's hold was tight. "Let me go," I screamed, frightened. Things *weren't* going to be different. I could feel it in the way Mom held on to me. "Let me go."

"Caitlynne," Cara called from somewhere in the dark.

"Virginia." Nana was close to Mom and me. "Let them stay here while you get settled at the lake."

"We're leaving, Cara," Mom called. "Are you coming?"

"Run, Cara," I screamed. "Run away!"

Mom's other hand slapped the side of my face. For a moment I was surprised. Stars that weren't in the night sky danced in front of my eyes. Mom pushed me ahead of her. Down the steps, into the dark.

"Cara," Mom called, her voice soft.

"Don't say anything," I yelled at my sister.

Mom hit me again, this time with her fist. The blow landed near my ear, and I wondered if I was bleeding because, for a moment, my skin felt all warm there.

"Virginia, please." Nana ran out behind us. Mom moved me this way and that, keeping me from my grandmother.

"Cara," she called. "Let's go home. I have dinner waiting."

A cold chill went down my spine. Mom never made dinner. Ever. I stumbled and fell to my knees. She pulled me up with a jerk.

"Don't do that again," she said, "or I'll beat the living hell out of you." I could tell by the way she was speaking that she was gritting her teeth.

"Let me go, Mom," I said. "You're hurting my arm."

"Virginia," said Nana. "Come inside. Let Caitlynne go, and you and I can have a beer and talk."

I wondered where Cara was hiding. Mom pushed me along. There wasn't much of a moon, and with all the trees, the yard was quite dark.

"Let's go," Mom said in a loud voice. "I'll be back for Cara. You and I can be a family alone, Caitlynne." Mom directed me down the side yard toward the front.

Nana stumbled behind us, trying to talk Mom into letting me go. When we got around to the front and I saw our old car, panic set in. I struggled to get away.

Mom knocked me away from her, never letting go. I felt like a yo-yo.

"Don't fight with me," she hollered. "You are my child. You will do as I tell you. Now get in the car."

Mom opened the door with one hand and held me tight with the other. How could she be so strong? I wondered.

"No, I don't want to go. I want to stay with Nana."

"Virginia, please," Nana's voice cried out. "Stay the night. We can talk about it in the morning."

A sound slap connected with my cheek.

"Get into the car."

"No." I felt, for a second, that I was fighting for my life.

Mom punched me in the back and I fell up against the car. She shoved me toward the open door, but I fought her.

Mom punched at me again and again. From far

away I heard Cara scream, "No!" Then she was there beside me, having come out of the dark into the near light of the car.

"Help," I said.

"Don't let her get you," Cara yelled at me. She took hold of one of my arms and pulled on me, but Mom smacked Cara away.

Mom turned on me with a fury.

"You're not taking me back," I screamed at her. "I'm staying here."

"Virginia, please. She wants to stay with me."

"You'll do as I say." Mom punched and slapped me with each word.

"I'm staying here! We're both staying here!" I swung back at Mom but missed her.

"How dare you?" Mom's voice echoed around the yard. "How dare you hit me?"

"Leave us alone," Cara said.

Mom's hitting grew worse. I covered my head, then moved toward the ground. Maybe I could crawl away.

Mom began to kick me. Then she turned on Cara, slapping and punching at my sister. I heard the hollow echoes of the blows that met Cara, heard her grunts.

Mr. Burd appeared. Mom turned like a monster and shoved the old man. He toppled, and I wondered if he would have fallen so easy if he had had all his fingers.

I grabbed at Mom's ankles, to stop her kicking. Her foot connected with my mouth, and I felt my lip split, then tasted blood.

"Run if you can, Cara," I said, but my voice was low, directed at the sandy driveway.

I heard another car pulling into the yard. Mom began screaming, and I couldn't understand any of what she said. She slapped and kicked and punched. Then, like a miracle, she was gone. I mean, I heard her, but she wasn't close by anymore. She wasn't striking out anymore. At least not at me.

Someone knelt close to where I was on the ground.

"Are you okay?" It was a man's voice, but not Mr. Burd's.

I looked from under my arm. A policeman looked back at me. "Where's my mom?" My voice was a whisper.

"She's at the car. My partner is talking to her over at the police car."

I looked up. Mom was still yelling, but she was a few feet away.

"They're my children," she shouted.

"We're not going back," I said. "No one can make us."

"Don't worry," he said. "You're safe now."

161

CHAPTER
TWENTY-THREE

The night seemed to drag by. Cara and I were hustled into the house, where two policemen came and talked to us about Mom and the summer alone. Nana nursed my lip. Aunt Margaret arrived a few minutes after Mom got calmed down and told Nana she would take us back to Orlando if the police thought she should. She could hardly look at me. Instead, she went with Mom to the hospital.

I had bad dreams all night. Once I woke up screaming. Nana came into the room to where I was, huddled next to Cara, and sat on the bed.

"It's okay," Nana said. "Caitlynne. It's all right. She's gone."

"She almost got us," I said.

"I never knew," Nana said. "I never knew it was so bad."

"It was worse," said Cara. "Tonight was nothing."

I swallowed at a lump in my throat.

"How could I not have seen?" Nana asked, and she wasn't talking to Cara or me.

"It's all right," I said.

"No, it's not," Nana said. "I should have seen and made things right. I knew something was wrong. I never thought it was like this."

"It's okay, Nana," I said.

She patted my back and left the room. I heard her call Uncle Ryan on the phone.

"It's not okay," Cara whispered at me, her breath warm in my hair.

A chill, like the one that had gone through me earlier, went down my spine again.

"What do you mean?" I asked.

"She'll get out of the hospital soon enough."

I felt sick to my stomach.

We were quiet a moment.

"You fought back," Cara said.

"Not too good," I said. "But yeah, I did. I wasn't going without a fight. I'm not ever going again without a fight." I thought for a moment more. "I'm not ever going back again, period."

Cara giggled a little. I did, too. I knew anybody seeing us laugh about me slapping at my mother wouldn't think it was funny.

Nana hung up the phone. She came and stood in the doorway. She was all dark because the light from the hall broke around her from the back.

"Your uncle will come first thing tomorrow. We'll talk about your staying here permanently." Nana took a step into the room, and both Cara and I sat up in bed.

"I'm sorry," she said again. And then she burst into tears.

"Nanny," I said, calling her the name I had used when I was much younger. I held my arms out to her.

Nana practically ran to the bed. She fell to her knees and wrapped her arms around me. Her hug hurt places on my back, but I didn't say anything. I just hugged my grandmother. And Cara did, too.

"I better get to bed," Nana said after a while. "Caitlynne, Cara. I love you both very much."

"I love you, too, Nana," we both said.

Nana left the room, closing the door partway behind her. A fat thread of hall light squeezed through the crack in the door. I was almost asleep when Cara said, "She could come back."

Her words woke me right up.

"She could come anytime and take us. She could do it all over again, like tonight."

I remembered Mom hanging on to my arm. I remembered her breath hot on my face. Underneath my head, my pillow sighed as I moved to get more comfortable.

"This is home," I said. "Nana said so."

"She'll be back," Cara said.

"We won't let her take us. We'll fight again." It was scary to say it, but I knew that I would fight again and again and again, if I had to.

"We could go back to the lake. We could hide there," Cara said.

I thought about it a moment. Then I shook my head, and my pillow rustled. "I don't want to do that. I want us to live here. Safe, with Nana. I like this feeling."

"Will we ever be safe?" Cara asked. I knew she wasn't really talking to me, more to herself. But I answered her anyway.

"If we stick together, we'll be okay. We can't let her push us around anymore."

I took a deep breath, then turned on my side. I lay awake for a long time, listening to the freezer in the hall hum, and wondering.

CHAPTER

TWENTY-FOUR

▼

The sun was just coloring the sky morning when I awoke. Already the house was warming up. Maybe it had never cooled off from the night before.

I got my sketch pad and pencils and, still dressed in my nightshirt, wandered around Nana's quiet house. I looked in on my grandmother. She was lying on her back, her mouth open in a snore.

In the kitchen I ate breakfast, a few cold biscuits with pancake syrup poured on top. I sat at the bar and gazed out the glass of the door. After I had eaten, I went and sat on the back step.

Thick dew dressed the yard. The bright green Spanish bayonet was covered with the tiny water droplets. The heavy rye grass was coated with wetness. The eastern sky was a strained blue, almost too pale to even notice. The horse pasture behind the shed looked like it was covered in a low cloud, there was so much dew.

What a picture, I thought. I started to take my things out to draw, but changed my mind. I stretched out my legs instead and flipped through my artwork. Tucked in the last page of the book was the picture I had been working on at the end of the school year. It was the one of Cara and me, standing on the lake, watching the sun.

What was wrong with this, I wondered. Even after all this time, the drawing still wasn't right. Something was missing. Was it Nana? Was it Mom?

And then I realized what wasn't right about my painting. It was the picture of me. The girl I had drawn was puny looking. She hadn't lived a summer trying to take care of her little sister. The girl I was staring at now would never be able to stand up to someone who was mean to her. The girl in the picture wasn't real.

I walked down the back steps and started around the house, going the way Mom and I had last night.

That girl *had* been me, I thought. At the beginning of the summer it was me. When had I changed? During the long weeks taking care of Cara and me? Or was it knowing Brandon, or the ride over to Nana's?

When I reached the front yard, I was startled to see

Mom's car sitting in the driveway. I stood for a moment, staring at it.

"She's gone," I said to the stranger in the painting. "And the next time she comes back, I'm going to be stronger still."

I'm saving this picture forever, I thought. I want to keep seeing how I used to be. All I had to do was wait and maybe I would find myself changed even more.

"Hey," called Cara from the front porch. "What are you doing?"

I turned around. There she stood, in her to-the-knees nightgown. Her hair looked ratty. I wondered how messed up it was in back.

"Waiting," I said. "Just waiting."

About the Author

Carol Lynch Williams is the author of several books for children, including two novels about the Orton family of New Smyrna, Florida: *Kelly and Me* and *Adeline Street*. A two-time winner of the Utah Original Writing Competition, she lives in Mapleton, Utah, with her husband and four daughters.